THE BEAT OF THE DRUM

Martin Waddell is widely regarded as one of the finest contemporary writers of books for young people. He has won many awards and was Ireland's nominee for the prestigious Hans Christian Andersen Award in 2000. Among his many titles are the novels *Tango's Baby*, *The Life and Loves of Zoë T. Curley* and *The Kidnapping of Suzie Q*. *The Beat of the Drum* is one of a trilogy of books set in Northern Ireland. The other books in the trilogy are *Starry Night*, which won the Other Award, was runner-up for the Guardian Children's Fiction Award and was shortlisted for the Young Observer Teenage Fiction Prize, and *Frankie's Story*. Martin Waddell lives with his wife Rosaleen in Newcastle, County Down, Northern Ireland.

*For a boy who planted a bomb
in August 1972, in the hope that he's
still alive to read it*

Books by the same author

Starry Night

Frankie's Story

Tango's Baby

The Kidnapping of Suzie Q

The Life and Loves of Zoë T. Curley

THE BEAT OF THE DRUM

MARTIN WADDELL

WALKER BOOKS
AND SUBSIDIARIES
LONDON · BOSTON · SYDNEY

Notice to all Readers

This book is a work of fiction. All characters are entirely fictitious and every care has been taken to obviate any accidental or unintentional identification with any living persons either directly or indirectly.

The Loyalist area portrayed in this book could be any large town in Northern Ireland. The setting is deliberately unspecific.

First published 1989 by Hamish Hamilton
under the name of Catherine Sefton

This edition published 2001 by Walker Books Ltd
87 Vauxhall Walk, London SE11 5HJ

2 4 6 8 10 9 7 5 3 1

Text © 1989 Martin Waddell
Cover illustration © 2000 Mark Preston

The right of Martin Waddell to be identified as author
of this work has been asserted by him in accordance with the
Copyright, Designs and Patents Act 1988

This book has been typeset in Sabon

Printed and bound in Great Britain by
The Guernsey Press Co. Ltd

British Library Cataloguing in Publication Data:
a catalogue record for this book is
available from the British Library

ISBN 0-7445-7824-8

CHAPTER ONE

"You berk, Hicky!" I said cheerfully.

"Berk yourself, Hanna!" said Hicky, grinning back at me. Hicky and Val Martin and I were down at the yellow swings, watching the sun flicker on the river. It isn't *that* great a river. If you swim in it you can get our version of the Black Plague, or worse.

"It's good though, isn't it?" said Hicky, displaying his brand new Walkman.

"Did you steal it?" Val said.

"Naw," said Hicky unconvincingly. "Paid cash, didn't I? The money I found down at the old houses."

"You stole it," I said.

I knew Val would be unhappy about it, and she was. She stood there with a pale moon-face on, blinking down at me through her heavy-framed glasses, her hand toying with the backrest on my wheelchair.

"If you found that money in the derelicts, you should take it to the police," she said stubbornly. She was trying to say what her dad would have said, but coming from a teenager it sounded a bit off-key. Pastor Martin is the preacher in the mission hall in Lochiel Street.

I thought Hicky was going to give her a mouthful, but he didn't. He ignored her instead, which must have been something to do with fear of her father.

"See you around, Hanna," he said to me, and he turned on his heel and went out of the playground.

"Where are you going, Hicky?" I shouted after him.

"Just naffing off," said Hicky, and he gave me a big grin. Then he slouched off down the road, making for the flats.

"Do you believe that he found that money he goes on about, Brian?" Val asked me anxiously.

"He says he did," I said.

Val made a face.

She took off the jacket of her suit, and slung it over my chair bag. My wheelchair gets everybody's rubbish, so people can push me around without having to carry things. It makes me into a kind of wheelie dustbin, enriched with marrow-bone jelly.

"Come on," Val said.

"Where are we going?" I said.

"Going to chuck you in the river, Brian!" she said.

We went rattling down the street, heading nowhere, for there was nowhere in particular to head. We made an odd couple, Val, a big handsome girl, in her heavy grey skirt and prim blouse buttoned high at the neck despite the fact that it was midsummer and hot, and me in my chair.

"He doesn't like me, does he?" she said, still thinking about Hicky.

I didn't say anything.

"Why doesn't he like me?" she said.

"I like you," I said, not very deftly avoiding the question. I do like her. I didn't want to annoy her.

"I know about you," she said, smiling. She has a nice smile when she lets it go.

"Well then...?" I said.

"I will tip you in the river, honest I will!" she said, and the conversation got away from Hicky, which pleased me well enough, because I didn't want to explain Hicky to her.

Hicky and I go back a long way. He more or less lived in our house when he was little. Anywhere Auntie Mae took me in my chair, Hicky came along too. He was a latchkey kid, I suppose, and my Auntie Mae is famous for picking losers. She was genuinely fond of Hicky when he was small, playing around with me. She still is fond of him, probably, although she'd never say so. He's a hopeless case, Hicky.

Val's something else again. She comes from her dad's posh house, and she has all the ideas from it packed into her. It's an odd bundle, Christian

7

Charity and the Good Book going hand-in-glove with Kick the Pope and Burn the Fenians … that's her dad's message when he's in the pulpit. He loves Catholics, that is what he says, he loves Catholics and Communists and Jews and Muslims – he loves them all because they are God's Creatures. It is *loving* them that makes him determined to fight for what-he-knows-is-right for them, whether they know it or not. If turning their faces towards the one true Jesus means saying things that hurt them then he has to do it, he has no choice, because his Bible tells him so.

Val is just like him. All God-is-love one minute, and black bitter Protestantism the next.

She's sixteen, seventeen nearly, same age as me, but she doesn't act it. The clothes don't help. The Martins keep her dressed like an old woman, in heavy clothes that no one else would wear, with sensible shoes and thick tights. Before she met me she hardly got out of the house at all, except to go to school, or visit country gospel halls with her father. Her big break for freedom came with the Joy Club. It is for the handicapped, and they had to let her go there to be a helper, because it counts as Good Works. That's where she met me. They can't object to her taking me wheelies because that's Good Works. I don't object either. It is a relief after years of being wheeled by Hicky.

Val taking over his wheelie duty didn't help with Hicky. He used to be about our place a lot, but now he doesn't come round so much. That's part

Val, and part me, and part the lot he has taken up with.

"It's hard to believe there is all the trouble, on a sunny day like this," Val said, as we bumped along the pavement by the river. "All the bombing and shooting."

"Yeah," I said.

"My dad says the Catholics will never give up, till the government lets the army at them," she said.

"Yeah," I said.

I'm used to her parroting her dad. I try not to let it get to me.

"Why don't they let the army finish the IRA off?" she said. "I don't understand."

We had pulled up at the traffic lights, waiting to cross over to the park.

"The army can't just go into Republican areas and shoot people," I said. "Being a Catholic isn't a capital offence."

"My dad says the army knows who the godfathers are," she said. "My dad says it would be all over in a week."

I didn't try telling her that her dad could be wrong. It wouldn't have done any good. For somebody of sixteen she hasn't grown up. What her dad says goes. The frightening thing is that she doesn't see anything odd in spouting Jesus-loves-me stuff one minute, and final-solution-politics the next.

"You want to watch that girl, Brian," my Auntie Mae said to me, after the first time Val

9

came round our house. "The good living ones are the worst."

"Why?" I said, because I hadn't seen that side of Val then.

"Because they can justify anything to themselves," she said. "Anybody who disagrees with them is in league with the devil!"

My Auntie Mae was right.

Val *is* like that, but at the same time she is kind and gentle and considerate. If anyone was in trouble, she would be the ideal person to turn to, so long as politics wasn't involved. Her dad has the same reputation.

Val's concern about Hicky wasn't a put-on. She was upset. By her dad's standards Hicky was on the downward path. She knew she had a duty to turn him away from it. I wasn't comfortable with the notion, because I didn't think she could cope. I was hoping we could stay off the subject, but as soon as we got inside the park it came right back into play.

Duggie was there. Duggie is one of my friends, not Val's. The first time she met him she lectured him about smoking, and he turned off her for good.

He came up to us.

"Seen Hicky's Walkman?" he said. "It's a goozer, that Walkman!"

"We don't know where he got the money to buy it from," Val said stiffly.

Duggie grinned at me, but said nothing.

"He says he bought it with the money he got

from the derelicts," I said in a half-hearted attempt to save the situation. The one hundred pounds Hicky is supposed to have found at the derelict houses has been around a long time as an alibi to cover all sorts of transactions involving Hicky and unaccounted-for cash. It doesn't cross his mind that people can add up! None of which would matter much, but if I can add it up, so can other people, and where we live that doesn't just mean the police. We have the paramilitaries to cope with as well.

"Yeah, he does!" said Duggie, straightening his little football hat. He wears his football hat in all weathers, and his woolly jacket with the badges. He must have every pin-on badge there ever was.

"Do *you* believe he found that money?" Val asked Duggie. She was intent on finding out, for Hicky's sake, not for her own.

Duggie looked at me and shrugged, as if to say: *Where did you dig this giraffe up?* What he actually said was: "It's got sod all to do with me."

"Hicky could get lifted by the police," Val said. "You know what happened last time."

"Yeah!" grinned Duggie. "Got away with it again, didn't he?"

Last time was when Hicky went shopping without a shopping bag. He had his big anorak on, the one with the cut-out in the pocket lining. Pop into the lining goes whatever Hicky is after, down through the hole into the bottom of his coat. Brilliant! It got him arrested of course, because he tried to walk out of the shop door about three times as thick around the bottom of the coat as he had been when he walked in. Hicky was for the high jump, but somebody must have put a word in for him with the police, because the case didn't get to court.

"We ought to do something about it," Val said stubbornly.

"*We?*" said Duggie.

"Yes. Us. We're supposed to be his friends."

"Are *you?*" said Duggie.

"Even if I'm not," she said, "*you* are. You and Brian, both of you."

I stirred uneasily. She was worked up about it, thrilled at the prospect of a soul-saved-for-Jesus. I've given up on Hicky's soul. I'm not sure that Hicky's soul is *involved*. He hasn't much sense and he pinches things like towel rolls, that aren't any use to him. I don't know what he pinches them for, and neither does Hicky, if you ask me.

"We ought to do something to stop him!" she said.

It was all clear and simple in her mind: *Do something*.

"We could break both his legs and put him in hospital," said Duggie, grinning wildly at her.

"You're trying to be funny," she said.

"Naw," he said. "I *am* funny."

Val froze.

"Hey! Hey!" I said. "Wait a minute. No call for you two to start fighting."

"I'm away off," Duggie said. "You stay and hold her hand."

And off he went.

"Why is he mad at me?" Val said, watching him go. "I'm only trying to help Hicky, you know that, Brian."

"Don't take it personally, Val," I said.

"It is personal," she said.

"Just calm down a minute," I said.

"I am calmed down," she snapped.

"Val?" I said.

"All right," she said, kicking the wheel of my chair. "It isn't your fault."

"You were only trying to help," I said lamely.

Guilt stirred in me. She was trying to help, and I wasn't.

Why not? Hicky needed helping, that was clear enough. So why wasn't I trying to help him?

"I wish I had your faith in people," I said.

"I wish you had too," she said, snatching game-set-and-match for Jesus by the blink of her eyes behind her heavy glasses.

JESUS SAVES – that is what it says in the big white letters on her dad's hall. It was very clever of me to sit there in my wheelchair thinking that was a cop-out, but when it came down to a real problem, like what to do about Hicky – my friend, not her friend, because she didn't even like him – when it came down to that, at least she was trying.

So where did that leave me?

Hicky was my friend. The whole early bit of my life was full of outings with Hicky and my Auntie Mae, going places, playing games, always the three

13

of us. Hicky doing this, Hicky doing that, with his skinhead haircut and the jeans with the backside out of them. I don't know why they didn't get him proper jeans ... nobody in the Hicky house seemed to mind what he did, or what he looked like. The only time I remember his mum at all was when we went to *her* house, over the ciggies. Hicky turned up on my Auntie Mae's birthday with a present of a packet of cigarettes. Of course, he'd pinched them from his mum. My Auntie Mae made him take them back. His mum gave him a tanning and Hicky was mad. He didn't come near our house for days. In the end he sidled back, and Auntie Mae arranged a big day out on the bus for us and it was all forgiven and forgotten.

Auntie Mae paid the bus fares. I don't think Mrs Hicky even knew he had been away.

My friend.

He hasn't changed much, he's still a ciggy pincher, but I have, and I felt guilty about not being the same as I was, Hicky's mate.

It made me feel mean.

I had to try to help him somehow. I couldn't leave it all to Val.

"You're right, Val," I said. "You're right and I am wrong, on this one."

She didn't say anything. She just beamed her Jesus-loves-me beam, looking down at me through her glasses, pale face all lit up.

It was very disconcerting.

CHAPTER TWO

Val and I mucked about in the park for a bit. I suppose it must have been about half-past four when we left, after the second tour round by the tennis courts.

I had a notion there was something Val wanted to see down there, or somebody, but she never said a word, and I didn't. I was happy to be out in the air, enjoying things, and not stuck in our stuffy front room.

My chair is the problem. My left front wheel has gone a bit wonky since Hicky crashed me down the steps at Apple Street. We were doing a bunk at the time, because Hicky had stolen some old woman's milk bottle from her step. It was childish stuff, and stupid, and I was mad at him, but I couldn't do anything about it because of the chair. Hicky stuck the milk bottle in my chair bag and headed for the hills, bonk-bonk-bonk down the steps, and my wheel got twisted. My Uncle Billy has been going to fix it for weeks, but he never gets round to it, and with the bent wheel I can't get far myself, not much further than the chip shop. Anyway it's much easier to get about when there is someone to push me.

It was also nice to have someone pushing me who wasn't likely to head into trouble of one kind or another, like Hicky or Duggie. You never know where you'll end up with them doing the pushing.

We bumped off out of the park, and then I spotted Hicky.

"Hold on!" I said. "There's Hicky."

"Where?" Val said.

Hicky was down the road from us. He was leaning against a doorway, just beside the Turnpike Off-licence, at the corner of Malt Street.

An army patrol was on its way by, and Hicky was busy looking the other way as the soldiers passed him. They were about twenty feet apart, walking slowly, close into the shop fronts, their rifles cocked and their heads on the swivel. Every so often one of those rifles goes off. They weren't a reassuring sight on our Good Protestant Streets. God alone knows what they make the Catholics feel like.

"Hicky looks as if he shouldn't be there," I said, beginning to feel anxious.

"What do you think is going on?" Val asked, slowing down, because she didn't want to be part of it.

"I get it!" I said.

"What?"

16

"His mate French is in the Turnpike loading up with beer cans, and Hicky is out there waiting for him," I said. "He's afraid his ma will catch him."

"Does Hicky *drink*?" she asked.

Only Val could say it and sound shocked! She had stopped altogether, and was peering up the road.

"I'll go down Major Street, where he won't see us," she said, and off we went, which wasn't what I'd planned, because I needed to know what Hicky was up to.

I was worried about Hicky, and more particularly about Hicky and French. Hicky boasts about the big deals French is in on. Mostly it comes down to joy-riding with another mate of his called Conrad Taylor. My Uncle Billy told me that the UDA had had words with French and Conrad Taylor, and when that happens you *know* you are in trouble.

UDA – that's the Ulster Defence Association, the protestant equivalent of the Provos ... well, kind of.

The UDA run a vigilante service, military courts and all, just like the Provos. The Provos blow off Catholic kneecaps, and the UDA blow off Protestant kneecaps, so everybody has an even chance.

Val was worried about Hicky's soul. I was worried about his kneecaps.

"Hold on, Val," I said. "I want to see what they're up to."

"Why?" she said.

I couldn't say: "In case French is in there

17

threatening somebody with a Stanley knife, and Hicky's keeping sentry outside," so I said: "Because," and left it there.

"See you, Brian Hanna," she said, not very happily. "For somebody who wants to be wheeled around all day, you are very demanding. It is time you got an outboard fitted."

We did a turn back down Major Street, but when we got to the Road, there was no sign of Hicky. I was relieved.

French and Conrad Taylor were up by the chippy, leaning on the window. Leaning on windows is what they do best. They had a six-pack apiece, no doubt paid for out of Hicky's elastic one hundred pounds.

"Push me up past those two till I see what they're doing," I said. "We're OK, Val. They're on the other side of the street."

It wasn't very bright of me, I suppose, but I was still thinking of the Hicky problem. If he was getting the money the way I thought he might be, by going on "jobs" with French and Taylor, then he needed helping. I don't know how I thought I could help him. I wanted to try.

So I got her to wheel me back up the Road towards the two at the chippy, which was foolish, because they come from the real world, those two, Big Boot Division.

They spotted us.

They came across the road.

"Hullo, darling," Conrad said to Val.

"Any friend of Hanna's is a friend of ours," French said. "Ain't that right, Legless?"

Then he squatted down on the pavement with his knees bent, right in front of my chair. He spread his arms out wide, and pretended to be a big bird.

"Flap-flap-flap!" he said. "Bet you wish you could fly, Legless."

Conrad held his beer can out to Val. "Have a drink?" he said.

"No, thank you," said Val, blinking at him nervously.

"No thanks?" said Conrad. "Well, thank *you* very much!"

"Are you going to let us pass?" Val said, giving him a scared-owl look through her glasses.

"Would we stop you?" French said.

Conrad took his beer can and held it over my head.

"Like a beer-bath, son?" he said.

"Leave him alone!" Val snapped.

She jerked the chair back, and for a moment I thought she was going to run me forward, slap into French's groin, but she didn't. She spun the chair round, and we headed back the way we'd come.

"Don't go up the side streets," I told Val. "They'd be after us."

"I have more wit than that," she said.

They shouted things after us, mostly about my legs, but they didn't bother following us. If Val

19

hadn't looked like a weird kid it might have been different, but I didn't tell her that.

Poor Val. She had gone pale. She was sick-scared looking. I was sick at myself, because it was my fault. I'd run her into it, knowing what they were like. I didn't bargain on a scene like that happening on the Road. I didn't think they'd bother.

"I'm sorry," I told her. "I shouldn't have walked you into that."

"Yes," she said.

"I should have known better," I said. "But I've had a sheltered life." I was trying to make a joke out of my chair, to divert her, although my chair is no joke really, when it comes to that sort of thing. The chair is a trap I'm in. I have to go where I am wheeled, and that depends on who is doing the wheeling.

"Listen," I said. "You're very good, coming all the way down here and wheeling me about like this. I don't want you getting annoyed by things like that. It *was* my fault. I should have guessed it might happen."

"My mum would have killed me, if she'd seen me with those two," Val said.

"Well, your mum would have been quite right," I said.

She got me home, and then she had to go. Mrs Martin says she has to be home in time for tea. It is one of the rules when Val comes out to do her Good Works. I don't think they really like her being out of the house at all but they reckon I am

the next best thing to a safe bet in our neighbourhood.

It isn't the sweetest place, our neighbourhood,
but it isn't the worst either, I suppose. My Uncle
Billy loves it. He has lived all his life in this town,
and the only big change in all that time was getting
an extension on the back of the house to make room
for me growing up. He's happy with his little house,
and our street, and Northern Ireland. He gets very
angry with the IRA for trying to blow it all up.

I could leave tomorrow, and so could my Auntie
Mae. She took Hicky and me out into the country
one day, and showed us the house where she and
my mum used to live when they were kids. It was
a bit of a dump, out in the country, and the roof
was off it, but you could see she loved it. She must
have loved my Uncle Billy a lot to leave it and come
to our street. I think she would still like to get back
to the country, out of this place.

I suppose I will leave here one day, if I get my A
levels. Go to a university somewhere, something
like that. Somewhere on the mainland, not too far
away. I have my life mapped out that way,
anyway. My map involves coming back to see
Auntie Mae and Uncle Billy, and Hicky even, and
Duggie, but it doesn't involve me living here with
them.

I don't think I could do that for the rest of my life.

I don't see why I should have to, the way things
are here.

CHAPTER THREE

My Uncle Billy was late home for his tea, so Auntie Mae put it in the oven. We had ours together in the back kitchen and when we were finishing, things got going in the street outside.

BAM! BAM! BAM!

"Oh Lord!" said my Auntie Mae. She is a tough, wiry little woman, and now she wandered through the hall door heading for the front of the house without any enthusiasm at all.

"It's only Ollie," I said.

"And his bloody drum!" she reported back, and she came back into the kitchen, slamming the door behind her, as if she could cut out the noise. Some hope! Ollie's drum is designed to rock the foundations of the world, and it does when it is bam-bam-bamming in the street outside your house.

William Lyon Temperance Young Defenders marching band were limbering up.

The Young Defenders meet in the band rooms

attached to the mission hall two nights a week, and
every so often they go out on a summer evening to
practise parading.

It was obviously one of their practise-parading
evenings. They have red hats and blue jackets and
white trousers. The red hats have red, white and
blue feather cockades on them. Ollie Leadbetter
has the big drum and then there are half a dozen
side drummers, and the rest have fifes.

I pushed myself out to our front to have a look
at them.

Ollie already had a sweat on, and he hadn't even
got going on the bamming. He saves his best bamming for Crown Street, where there are four
Catholic houses. He likes to let them know he is
there.

Hicky came over to me, dressed in his band uniform, with his thin arms poking out of the sleeves
of a blue jacket that was too small for him. He was
all wrists and ankles, and on the ankles he had his
grey school socks, not like the other bandsmen
who were wearing white.

"You've got your socks wrong, Hicky!" I told
him.

"Dry up, Hanna," he said.

Then he handed me his fife.

"Have a tootle on the thingy," he said. "No, not
that way!" And he showed me how to work my
fingers.

"Here, friend Hicky! In line!" shouted Mr Malcolmson. He's the band leader. He organizes them.

23

"Don't let him spot your socks!" I told Hicky. He took his fife from me and scooted out on to the road.

Hicky can play the fife well, which puzzles me, because I don't know how he reads the music. He can't read much else, only small words. He used to like it well enough when my Auntie Mae read us stories when we were little, but he didn't seem to pick up the shapes of the words. It started to go wrong at primary school, and just got worse and worse after that. He gave up. He used to let me read to him. My Auntie Mae says he is dyslexic, and the school should have been able to sort him out in a special class, but I don't think Hicky made it to school regularly enough to get anything sorted out. He can't read words, but he must be able to read music, and I don't understand that. Maybe he does it by ear. Two of his cousins are in the Young Defenders, so it is possible that he got in on their say so, and has been kidding his way along ever since, pretending he can read music when he can't.

"Right!" shouted Mr Malcolmson. "Cleaver Street, and then the Road, then down to Crown Street where you do your encore, then round the back, Major Street, back to the hall and disperse. Off you go!"

Tum-tum-tum went the side drummers. French was in the middle, looking proud of himself. He has such long legs that the band trousers were up around his ankles, but he had white socks on. Hicky must have loosened his belt, because his white trousers were dropping over the tops of his black shoes, hiding the grey school socks.

The *tum-tum-tum* set them off, and then the fifes came in, sharp and reedy, and the band was on the march with Mr Malcolmson striding along the footpath beside them as though he owned it, his back military stiff.

"Coming?" Duggie said. He was out in front of his house, which is next door to us.

"All right," I said, and off we went.

I'm not great on following bands, but I didn't fancy staying at the house. The bands always annoy my Auntie Mae, and I didn't fancy sitting in to discuss it with her. The marches bring things to a head in our house, because you can't get away from the banging of the drums, and pretend they aren't there. My Auntie Mae and Uncle Billy have their differences, but they don't have rows, except about the bands. She says they ought to be stopped parading and he says he'd like to get his hands on any politician that tried to stop them, because if we haven't the right to walk the streets of our own town, then what have we got? It goes on and on like that. He wants to know what we fought the Hitler war for if it wasn't Freedom and Democracy and when he gets to that bit she just gives up. It isn't weakness on her part, it is strength. She knows how much a few words from her could hurt him and she isn't prepared to do that.

Duggie really likes the bands. He was skipping about behind me like a big kid which, combined with my dodgy front wheel, made for some narrow misses.

There was the usual taggle of little kids behind the band, and we jolted off the pavement and joined them, tucking in behind a group with an Ulster Red Hand flag. There were four big RUC men at the end of our street, standing round their armoured car. One of them did a mock dance as the band went by, and his mates started joking him about it. Conrad Taylor was up front, with his whirly stick, and he did his whirl and laid the stick along his arm, pointing left, and the band wheeled into Cleaver Street.

BAM! BAM! BAM! went Ollie on his drum, going past the Nearys' house. The Nearys are Catholics. Their curtains didn't stir. They'd be in the back. Some of the kids we were with scraped Sean Neary's old beat-up car as we were going past it, just out of fun.

"They're really good!" Duggie said, jigging about.

"Why aren't you in it still?" I said.

"Old Malcolmson turfed me out," Duggie said.

"What for?" I asked.

"Put my foot through a side drum, kicking Winston Orme," Duggie said.

"Mr Malcolmson goes mad if you muck about in the band rooms," I said.

William Lyon Temperance Young Defenders is Mr Malcolmson's baby. It used to be William Lyon Temperance only, and then the Young

Defenders started up at the flats, run by Andy Cloakey. Andy ran them so well that he disappeared with the funds, and the next thing was a UDA deputation led by Ollie Leadbetter's dad, Stan, on Mr Malcolmson's doorstep. The UDA man saw the Young Defenders as a way of keeping French and his friends in line, and they talked Mr Malcolmson into a merger. After that it was William Lyon Temperance Young Defenders, with the blessing of the UDA, and everybody was happy. Everybody except Andy Cloakey, that is. Rumour has it that he is living in Leicester with no kneecaps.

That is the way things are run around here, for God and Ulster. It's not the same everywhere in Northern Ireland; it depends very much on the quality of the local paramilitary leadership. Round here is Stan Leadbetter's command area, and he makes sure things happen the way he wants them to. That goes for things like there *being* a band to keep the hard nuts off the streets, and also the UDA's brand of law and order, where no one is allowed to step out of line.

Tum-tum-tum went the drums, and we were back out on the Road, heading for the river. The sun was striking silver lights on the water, what there was of the water. You could see all the mud around the main channel baking, with things people had chucked into the river sticking out of it.

"Hicky's old trolley is there still," I said, pointing at it. It was an old supermarket trolley, wheels up. Hicky got out as far as it one day for a bet. When he got back his jeans were niffy with sludge and I don't know what. Somebody should tell Greenpeace about it.

"Let's catch them up!" Duggie said.

The band wheeled into Crown Street.

BAM! BAM! BAM! BAM! BAM! BAM! BAM! went Ollie Leadbetter, on the big drum. Conrad held up his stick and everyone stopped.

BAM! BAM! BAM! BAM! BAM! BAM! BAM! went Ollie.

They were halfway down Crown Street opposite the only four houses that weren't displaying flags. Don't ask me how Catholics got in the four houses, I don't know. Protestants sell to Protestants round our way. It keeps the ghetto spirit intact.

Ollie stopped bamming, and the side drums did a slow beat.

Tum-tum-tum-tum.

"Wait for it!" Duggie said, grinning.

Malcolmson gave the signal, and off went the fifes.

Straight into "The Sash".

They moved off down to the end of the street, then a turn, then back up again giving *BAM! BAM! BAM! BAM! BAM!* outside the four Catholic houses, with everybody stopped. Then the side drums did a roll, and in came the fifes again. We were off up the street, with all the kids skipping about, past the big King Billy on the gable, and out on to the Road.

28

"Look there," Duggie said, grinning.

A Catholic woman had come out of the last of the four houses, just as we were turning on to the Road. She didn't look happy. She stood there with her arms folded, for the benefit of her Protestant neighbours. They were all at their doors, where they'd been watching the band. None of them paid any attention to her.

"You'd think they'd move off somewhere," Duggie said. "Back to the Republic where they belong."

"I suppose they will," I said.

"The Catholics took over down below," he said, meaning further down the Road, which is Provo land. "They needn't think they're setting up their Republic here."

The Catholic woman was kneeling down, inspecting her four foot of front garden. One of the kids following the band had tipped a flower pot off her window ledge, and it lay smashed up on the ground.

"Hey, missus!" Duggie shouted.

The woman looked up.

"No Pope here, missus," Duggie shouted, and he gave her the fingers.

A big man came out of one of the nearest Protestant houses at the double.

"Get your bum out of here!" he shouted at Duggie.

"Bum yourself!" said Duggie.

The big man went red.

"None of your lip, son!" he said. "On your way."

Duggie stood there, looking at him.

"Come on, Duggie," I said. "Wise up."

"We know who you are," Duggie said to the big man. Then he turned away and started pushing me up the Road.

"I'm as good a Protestant as you are any day," the big man shouted after us.

"We know you!" was Duggie's parting shot.

The big man went back into his house.

"That put the wind up him rightly," Duggie said, with some satisfaction, though his neck had gone red inside his collar. I suppose from Duggie's point of view he had scored a goal.

I didn't say a thing. The big man could have pummelled Duggie into pavement pie if he'd had a mind to, but Duggie's "We know you" had an Ulster resonance that was all its own.

"He'll find a brick through his window, one of these nights!" Duggie muttered.

"*Is* he a Protestant?" I said.

"Bloody Fenian!" Duggie said. "Popehead."

"He came out of one of the Protestant houses," I said. "They had a Union Jack out the upstairs window."

"Then he should know what side his bread is buttered," Duggie said, gaining in confidence and volume the further we got from the actuality of the big man glowering down at him. "And if he doesn't know, he'll find out soon enough."

I thought about arguing the point, but it would

have been hopeless. I'd only have found myself abandoned in my chair, with a long wheel home to come.

I couldn't put up with Duggie at all, if he was brighter. He doesn't really know what he means when he shouts. Name-calling Catholics is just a thing Duggie does, like kicking beer cans. If he lived somewhere else, he'd be name-calling some-one else. It is the ones who *know* what they are doing and keep on doing it who worry me, and they are on both sides of the religious game.

The band was back on the bridge, tootling away on their fifes. The sky was all soft and glowy with the sun going down – what my Auntie Mae calls a "sun-egg" – and the kids following the band were happy. They were shouting and skipping about and waving their flags. People were out at their doors watching the band come across the bridge and chatting to the neighbours. All the houses had their flags fluttering and the thing about it being a community celebration seemed to make a bit of sense – so long as you didn't listen to the words the kids were shouting, or read the slogans they'd put up on the walls.

There are times when it sickens me.

"Lost your tongue, Hanna?" Duggie said, scuffing his boots on the kerb, which was red, white and blue, because of the season.

"No," I said. "Let's go home."

"Awright," Duggie said.

Some of the confidence had been taken out of

him by the big man's outburst. I wasn't sorry. It needed saying. I have tried with Duggie, but I don't get anywhere. So far as Duggie and the others are concerned, I'm a kind of king's fool in my chair, given licence by being so obviously different that they don't have to listen to what I say.

Probably it is just as well. If they didn't treat me as a joke, things might get serious.

"You're British," my Uncle Billy said to me when we were arguing about something. "You're loyal to the Crown. You couldn't be loyal to the Crown if you were a Catholic."

That about summed things up for Billy, and Duggie, and Hicky and more or less everybody round here.

Loyalty to the Crown means loyalty to the Protestant Crown, so how could a Catholic be included?

"You want to watch out, talking like that, or people will take you for a bloody Republican," Billy said to me. I forget what the conversation was about. The EEC probably. Billy knows that the Treaty of Rome was engineered by the Pope to force Ulster into an All Ireland Catholic Republic. All that nonsense about France and Germany getting together so there won't be a third war in Europe and free trade across the frontiers, and a common European heritage ... it's all a smoke screen. The EEC is a device to allow the Pope to rule Ulster in place of the Queen.

Billy knows it, because every Euro-election he

gets told it, again and again and again. Westminster MPs who appear otherwise to be sane and rational beings get up on their platforms and tell him about it, and Billy believes them.

It was a celebration of that kind of paranoia that the band on the bridge came down to, the skipping children with their banners, and the neighbours out at the street doors, waving as the *bam-bam-bam* went by.

The demented beating of Ollie's drum echoed up and down the Road, and round the side streets, but it wasn't a heartbeat, although it made the blood race.

It was the *bam-bam-bam* of something waiting to burst.

CHAPTER FOUR

Nine o'clock the next morning and Billy was still upstairs fast asleep, although my Auntie Mae had long since departed for her work. It was one of Billy's days off, but he didn't get lying about for long.

Bang-bang-bang went the door.

It was Stan Leadbetter, plus two.

The two were two I didn't know, but they looked like the heavy brigade.

"Your Uncle Billy in, son?" Stan asked.

"Up in bed," I said.

"Pitch him out of it!" Stan said, and he came into our front room. He didn't sit down. He just stood there with his two sidekicks, one on each side of him in their dark glasses.

Uncle Billy must have heard him.

He came downstairs, stuffing his shirt inside his trousers.

"You hear about the cops last night, Billy?" Stan said.

"Naw," my uncle said.

"They came and had a look round the band rooms at the mission hall," Stan said. "They pretended they were after one of the young lads for something."

"Hicky?" I said.

I should have kept my big mouth shut. Stan's attention swivelled back to me.

"Hicky?" he said. "You could be right, son."

I didn't know what he meant. There was something unwholesome in the way he said it.

"Hicky," he said to his sidekicks. Then his attention turned back to me.

"You," he said. "Out."

"Go in the back, Brian," Billy said. He didn't sound too pleased, but he didn't sound all that worried either.

Stan shook his head.

"Go out to the *front*, son," he said. And then he added: "Little pitchers have big ears," which set the two sidekicks grinning.

"OK," I said. "I'm going." I didn't feel all that happy about it. The local paramilitaries arriving in your front room and ordering you out isn't calculated to please, from where I'm sitting.

"He can fairly get about in that thing, can't he?" Stan was saying to Billy, as I went out of the door.

There was another one of them, dark glasses and forage cap, presumably UDA, watching in the street outside our house. He gave me a nod of recognition as I came out, but he didn't say

35

anything. He was leaning on our little front wall, in front of Auntie Mae's geraniums.

I didn't like the atmosphere, so I wheeled myself out of the way down to the foot of the street.

I didn't have to wait long.

The two sidekicks came out of the house and joined the third one. They went off together.

Then Stan and Billy came out.

They seemed very pally all of a sudden. I didn't even know that Billy *knew* Stan Leadbetter, except in the way that everybody knows him because he is our local generalissimo. The way they were buttering each other up you'd have taken them for long term leaseholders in each other's pockets.

Stan patted Billy on the back and shook his hand, and Billy wagged his tail at him, if you know what I mean.

"Round about eleven, Billy," Stan said, "All right?"

"No problem," Billy said.

Stan went off. He had a light tan jacket on him, leather, a white shirt, and a red, white and blue tie, moccasin shoes, and the obligatory black glasses. He looked like a cross between a TV evangelist and a tic-tac man.

What had Billy got himself into?

I went back to the house. He was sitting in the kitchen at the table, drinking a cup of tea.

"Well?" I said.

"Well, what?" he said.

"What did they want?"

"Nothing," he said.

"Nothing?" I said.

"Nothing."

"*Nothing?*"

"Nothing," he repeated, putting down his cup.

"That's a lot of fuss about *nothing*," I said, not to be put off.

"So far as you are concerned, nothing is happening and nobody's been here," he said. "Is that understood?"

"If you say so."

"I am saying it," he said.

"Well, that's fine with me," I said.

"And not a word to *her*," he said, with a nod of his head, vaguely indicating the bedroom upstairs where my Auntie Mae wasn't, but could safely be assumed to be for the purposes of the conversation.

He stood up.

"I'm going out for a while, doing things with the van," he said. "You don't know what I'm doing and you don't know where I am and you don't know when I'll be back. Understood? And in case you were thinking it, you don't *want* to know, either."

I looked at him. He is about five foot six in his cotton socks, with a fleck of grey in his hair, and a face like a fifty-year-old spaniel. He wears bifocals which are supposed to help with his myopia.

"Sounds like James Bond," I said.

"You're damn funny, Brian," he said, and off he went. He didn't seem too happy, but on the other hand he didn't seem too unhappy, either. He was all hyped up.

I was left wondering what Stan wanted with my Uncle Billy and his dingy British Telecom van. Normally Billy wouldn't have the van on his day off, but he'd got hold of it somehow, or he was getting hold of it. Wheels within wheels.

Billy isn't in the Ulster Defence Association, or any of the other Protestant organisations, so far as I know. The UDA is the upfront one. There are a lot of other sets of initials that get used from time to time, when somebody is found with his brains blown out in a quarry, for instance. Then it will be UFF – Ulster Freedom Fighters – or UVF – Ulster Volunteer Force – or any other set of initials anyone can think up. Whether or not they have separate membership isn't clear except to the people on the inside. There are lots of people who aren't in any organisation, but if there was any action they'd be on the barricades. Up to now, I'd taken my Uncle Billy for one of those. In a street like ours practically the entire civilian population can be counted on that way.

I'm not one of them, and I suppose that must be down to my Auntie Mae.

She brought me up British, all right. She is Protestant and British, although she doesn't wave a Union Jack about it. She's as British as Billy any day, but to him being British means other things. Being British means *not Irish* and being Protestant means *not Catholic*. It is all not, negative, and muddled up with our history, but it gives him a clear identity. Uncle Billy identifies with the people around him, but Auntie Mae can't, not any more.

She loves him, I know she does. She didn't just marry him, she meant it. She says back in those days they still banged the drum, but it was a kind of routine thing, nobody took much notice. It was only later it got really bad, and what happened changed Billy more than it changed her.

He never got over my mum and dad.

Their blood stained him.

He got really bitter after that, and the God and Ulster bit took him over. She turned to me, I suppose, because I was the left-over, the someone-to-look-after which is always the important thing with her.

He started hating, and because he started hating, and she couldn't stop him, she went the other way. She did all she could to stop *me* hating, to make me understand that it wasn't a simple two-sided problem ... she didn't betray him, she was with him when he needed her, but at the same time she tried to show me other things, other ideas.

As far as I am concerned her ideas won. She's always been stronger than Billy, really. Always been more a part of my life, anyway. But because of *that* – what happened to my mum and dad – and all the other things that have happened since, it must have been difficult for her. She didn't fight with Billy, she never contradicted him when he got spouting about Catholics this and Catholics that

39

and the British Government selling us down the river, but she inched her way just the same towards the idea that people come before anything else.

It's an odd feeling, living with her in the middle of all this bubbling feeling, the way we do, and *not* being a part of it in the way that my Uncle Billy is, and Duggie is, and Val is, and most of the people I know are.

I felt still enough a part of it *not* to see Uncle Billy's dingy British Telecom van parked just opposite the band rooms attached to the mission hall, when I took myself wheelies for chips at midday. Uncle Billy and two other men I didn't know were doing a passable imitation of sorting out some underground cables.

There are some things it is wiser not to see on a sunny street.

CHAPTER FIVE

After I'd eaten my chips, Val came.

She was all wired up, full of stories she'd heard about the police raid on the band rooms. Mr Malcolmson had been up to her house complaining about the RUC using local joy-riders as an excuse to go rampaging. Her dad had been on to the RUC, and he was making a big number of it, threatening to drag in the Northern Ireland Office.

"What were the police looking for?" I said, because that interested me, particularly with my uncle sitting down the road pretending to mend a cable that was directly outside the premises in question. Maybe it was a way for the UDA to keep an eye on the band rooms in case the police came again, but I didn't know that.

"You know very well they'll use any excuse to search in Loyalist areas," she said indignantly. "If this was a Catholic area you wouldn't see a policeman for miles. But down here it is different."

"And there's a war on," I said sarcastically.

"The police must have had a tip-off from somewhere," she said. "I wouldn't like to be in the shoes of the one who is talking, if his name gets about."

"How do you know there was a tip-off?" I said.

"It's obvious, isn't it?" she said. "You know what happens, Brian. My dad says the police get a hold on somebody, for an ordinary offence, and they use that as a lever to make the person inform for them."

"I don't think this was like that," I said. "It was just an ordinary search operation, to see if anybody had been hiding stuff down at the band rooms."

"Is that what you think?" she said, indicating that her dad didn't.

"The way I heard it, Mr Malcolmson kept the police talking at the door, whilst half a dozen of the Young Defenders made off over the back wall down to the dump," I said. "I don't know what they had with them, if anything, but if they have been hiding stuff in the band rooms that is their own lookout."

"It was police harassment, Brian," she said. She'd obviously been sitting in the corner listening to Mr Malcolmson agreeing with her dad.

I could imagine her dad on the subject: "The IRA are out to bomb us and burn us. They're killing Protestants, UDR men and policemen and judges and anybody they take a fancy to. That's where the war is in Ulster, and that is where our

42

Security Forces ought to be."

"My dad says the police pick on young Protestants like Hicky," she said. "It isn't fair."

"Yes," I said. There was no point in trying to argue with her dad by proxy. He's made himself a large public profile by sounding off about the Police and the Northern Ireland Office and Dublin Interference and the Betrayal of Protestantism.

"It is supposed to be a Protestant police force!" she said.

"No, it's not," I said wearily.

"Well, if it's not, it *should* be!" she said. "The Protestants are on their side trying to hold this country together. My dad says if the RUC want to go smashing things they should go through a few of the priests' houses. They might find more there than nuns with rosary beads."

She was such a big simple soul, trapped in her ultra-neat grey suit, parroting all the stuff she'd been weaned on, sitting at the foot of her father's pulpit. It wasn't her fault if she believed it all, but I couldn't help wondering what would happen if she ever stopped to think about it for herself.

"My dad wants to talk to Hicky," she said, suddenly switching her ground.

"Why?" I said.

"He doesn't want any trouble at the mission hall," she said. "He needs to know what Hicky and his friends were up to, or if it was just the RUC using them as an excuse. So he wants to see Hicky, like *now*. I'm sure my dad can help him, Brian."

She meant it. To Val, Pastor Martin was the nearest thing to Christ Risen on Earth.

"*Jesus saves,*" I said, and regretted it instantly. I'd hurt her. She was doing her thing, and all I could do was make cheap cracks about religion.

"Yes," she said. "Yes, He does!"

Which is how we wound up spending what felt like the warmest day of the year plodding round dusty pavements to Save Hicky for Jesus.

We ended up down at the derelicts, the scene of Hicky's supposed one hundred pound discovery.

There are six of the derelicts, in a row. They are little houses, with breeze blocks filling up the doorspaces, and the windows. Everybody has been writing the usual messages about God and Ulster and the UDA and what the Pope can go and do with himself on the breeze blocks. The writing is about the only sign of life left on the street, barring the parked cars. There'll be even more room for cars when they finish knocking down the houses.

We got into the yard at the back of number 6, and Val pulled away the sheeting Hicky had put up to cover his way in.

"Is it safe?" she said, peering in.

"No," I said.

"Brilliant!" she said.

"Push me in with you," I said.

Hicky's entry port let into what had been the back kitchen, once. You could see where the pipes had run, although they had long since disappeared to some scrap-merchants along with all the other

44

fittings, and the lead off the roof.

"Hicky?" I called.

"Somebody might hear us," she said.

"Yeah," I said. "Hicky might."

We made our way into the front room. There were some old boxes there, and a bit of Hicky litter, with some girlie pictures that Val made out she didn't see, or didn't care about if she did see them. I didn't comment on them because I felt awkward about it. I doubt if they had any pictures of scarlet women like that in Pastor Martin's house, Old Testament or no Old Testament.

"Let's go," Val said.

"What about up there?" I said.

"There's no way I'm clambering up there in my good clothes," she said. "It looks dangerous to me."

She was right. The staircase was long gone, just a zig-zag torn pattern up the remaining plaster on the walls, but the hole in the ceiling it had once passed through was still there. Somebody like Hicky could have skellied up the wall and hidden in one of the two postage stamp bedrooms above.

"What if he is up there asleep?" I said.

"Come off it," Val said. "He's not. You know he's not."

Well, I didn't know. I knew he wasn't at his house, because we'd called there, and I knew he wasn't in his usual places, because we'd covered most of them, but I didn't know what he might have been up to, which could have included drinking, swallowing or sniffing whatever he could get his hands on. That *might* lead to him lying on the floor upstairs sleeping something off on a sunny afternoon. There was no way of knowing. I'd no way of knowing that he *did* drink, swallow or sniff things, either, but he always talked as if he did.

"He goes up there," I said uneasily.

"Well, I'm not going up there, and you *can't*," she said, leaning against the wall and peeling away the wallpaper with her finger.

One layer, that is. There was layer upon layer of old plaster and wallpaper, all peeling and crumbly, with roses and leaves on it. Behind that was a kind of pink stuff, and green behind that, and the whole mess had damp running down it from the leadless roof … which was mostly tileless as well.

A firm was hired by the council to demolish the whole row. There is big money in demolition jobs, and apparently the owner of the firm refused to pay up when Stan Leadbetter's UDA men came asking for protection money. Shortly after that, one of the workmen got shot at, coming away from the houses, and the rest all downed their breaking tools and walked off the job. That's why what remains of the row of houses is still there.

That's the way the story goes, anyway. It may not be true. There are a lot of stories like that, both sides of the divide. Neither the Provos nor the UDA bother to deny them. It pays to advertise, I suppose, and a job left uncompleted is just that – an ad for paying your protection money when the nice man comes to offer you on-site security that you didn't know you needed.

"Come on, Brian," Val said. "I don't like it here. Let's go."

We went.

"If you find Hicky, you are to send him up to my dad," Val said, when she was bumping me back up the road.

"I'll do that," I said, feeling helpless, and in a funny way annoyed at her.

Hicky was *my* friend, even if he was a nutcase. I wanted it to be me that helped him, not Val or her dad ... but her dad was probably the only one who *could* help him, if it meant sorting things out with the police. So why did I resent it? I don't like Pastor Martin or what he stands for, that was it, I suppose, that and the feeling that I was a spectator, when I should have been doing things, helping things to get better, some way.

I'd love to do something to make it all better, but I can't think of anything that would. That's what makes it feel so hopeless.

Hope.

If I could find hope somewhere, then I'd fight for it.

Fighting is what they're all doing already! Fighting isn't going to do any good. Maybe the only hope is to keep on thinking *right* things, in the middle of it all, like Auntie Mae with her people-first talk.

I wish that I could find the words to change

people like Val and Duggie and Hicky and my Uncle Billy, to stop them being a part of Pastor Martin's God-and-Ulster game. If I couldn't change them, how could I even hope to change the others, the really committed ones, the UDA and the Provos and the politicians, all raving on about patriotically dying for the cause, *either* cause – red, white and blue, or green, white and gold.

I let Val bump me along, listening to her talk, and getting madder and madder at myself for being ineffectual, and faced with things I couldn't begin to cope with. I was in a bad mood by the time we got to Cleaver Street, and what I found there didn't make it any better.

The police had Cleaver Street cordoned off.

Someone had decided to strike another blow for Protestant Ulster.

There was a bomb on the window-sill at Sean Neary's, the one Catholic house on the street.

CHAPTER SIX

There were three police Land-Rovers in Cleaver
Street, one at the far end, and two at Neary's end,
though a bit away from the house. They had tapes
across the street, and all the neighbours were lined
up along them, waiting for their houses to be
blown up.

"Where is it?" I asked Neil Williamson. Neil
lives in the flats. He's a big kid, and he's in the
Young Defenders with Conrad Taylor, and Hicky
and French.

"Neary's window-sill," he said.

"Don't see it," Val said.

"Old bit of pipe, with the ends stuffed up," Neil
said.

"How do they know it is a bomb?" Val said.

"How do they know it *isn't*?" I said.

A big policeman came up to the crowd. "Everybody back, now," he said. "Move along, please.
Somebody could get hurt if that thing goes off."

Nobody moved. That isn't exactly true. The crowd drifted back when he said it, but only a yard or two, and as soon as he turned away they all came back.

"We shouldn't be here," Val said nervously. "Come on."

"I want to see what happens," I said.

"Brian...?" she said, looking down at me from a great height as usual, pale and anxious.

"Your dad won't know," I said.

"My dad will," she said. "He'll be down here in a minute."

She was probably right. Somebody would have been bound to tip him off. Pastor Martin always turns up when there's trouble. He's very good that way. He can talk rings round the police and they're less likely to lose the bap when he's there, because it all goes down in his notebook, and they are liable to find themselves famous on television afterwards.

Mr Malcolmson came up and started talking to the young policeman who was fixing the tapes.

"Come on, everybody stand back!" he said.

He was doing his sergeant major bit, as though he'd never left the army. He was in his element barking orders, a real law-and-order man. Nobody paid any attention.

"What about the cat?" Miss McCann said.

She's the old woman who lives with her sister Nessie, three doors up from the Nearys' house. I don't know why she's called "Miss McCann" and the other Miss McCann is called "Nessie". Miss McCann used to have a job in the wages office at Dunne and Gilmours, when there was a Dunne and Gilmours, so maybe it is a hangover from that. Nessie has a bad chest, from working in Coney Mill.

"What cat, Miss McCann?" asked Mr Malcolmson.

"Nessie's cat," she said. "On the wall. The black and white one."

Right enough there was a cat on the wall at McCann's house, sunning itself on their front wall. I didn't know they had a cat. It was only about ten metres from Neary's window-sill where the bomb was, if it was a bomb and not just a message for the Nearys, telling them to get out. They'd had their windows done a few times, and Sean Neary kept a hurley stick by the door to repel invaders, though I didn't know if he'd ever had to use it. It probably was just a message, but nobody knew that, and I don't suppose anybody felt like picking it up to find out.

"Well, call the cat, then!" said Mr Malcolmson.

"Skewball! Skewball!" called Miss McCann.

Skewball didn't take a blind bit of notice.

"Get it some food," suggested Mr Malcolmson.

Mrs Archer went into her house, and came out with a milk bottle. She put the milk in a saucer, and set it up on her wall.

"Everybody stand back so that the cat can see it!" ordered Mr Malcolmson.

"Skewball! S-k-e-w-b-a-l-l!" yelled Miss McCann.

The old cat wasn't interested. It was stretched out sleepily on top of the wall.

Nessie McCann came up.

"S-k-e-w-b-a-l-l!" she yelled. "Puss-puss-pussy!"

"Go and fetch it, Annie," Mrs Archer said to Miss McCann.

"S-k-e-w-b-a-l-l!" yelled Miss McCann. I didn't know her real name was Annie.

"Go and fetch it," said Mrs Archer again.

"I'll go," said Nessie anxiously.

"Indeed and you will not!" said Miss McCann, and she grabbed hold of her sister to stop her.

"Now, *ladies*," said Mr Malcolmson. "No need to panic."

"It's not your bloody cat!" Nessie said. She was all worked up. I reckon it must have been specially *her* cat, and Miss McCann just put up with it.

The policeman came over. Not the big cop that ordered us all off. This was the cop who had been tying the tape.

"What's the matter, love?" he said to Nessie.

"It's Skewball!" said Nessie, looking as if she was about to burst into tears.

"Nessie is worried about her cat," Mr Malcolmson said, rallying to her cause.

"It'll mind out for itself, love," the policeman said.

"How can the cat mind out for itself if it is blown up?" Nessie said.

"Go on, mister! You fetch it," said Mrs Archer.
The policeman didn't look pleased.

"Sorry, love," he said.

"You're all the same! No bloody good!" said Nessie.

"Now, Nessie, I'm afraid the officer is right," said Mr Malcolmson, putting in his tuppenyworth for the authorities. It must be the military training.

"What is the world coming to if a poor innocent cat gets butchered over a bunch of Republicans like the Nearys?" said Miss McCann.

There was a general mutter of agreement, and some character at the back shouted out, "Is it a *Protestant* cat?"

Everybody laughed, including the cop, but excluding old Nessie.

"Poor woman," Val said. "Can somebody not do something to help her with her wee cat?"

Everybody was getting at the policeman. I know if I had been him there is no way I would have gone up to that house to fetch Nessie's cat, if it was stupid enough to sit down beside a maybe-bomb. *Bang* goes the cat, and *bang* goes the policeman. Which sounds funny, but it is *real*. People have been killed before now doing things like that, and we've all seen the pictures. The policeman would have seen more than most. They are the ones who have to go round with the black plastic bags scraping up the remains after an explosion, and it is the sort of thing that leaves a mark beyond the blood on the wall and the bits in the bag.

Then I had a brainwave.

"Chuck a stone at it!" I said.

"Eh?" said Val.

"Chuck a stone at the old cat. That will shift it."

"You'll do no such thing!" said Nessie. "That's *my* cat."

"Hold on, Nessie," said Mr Malcolmson, brightening up at the prospect of action. "The lad's right. Trust young Hanna to have the answer."

"Find a stone!" somebody shouted, and the next minute they were in the wee gardens, hoking.

"Mind the cat now!" said Miss McCann. "Nobody hurt it!"

Mr Malcolmson got one of the stones, and he chucked it. It whizzed off the pavement near the cat, but he didn't score, and somebody shouted something about another miss for the artillery, which started the laughing again.

Then the policeman took one, and he walked a bit nearer, being inside the tape, and let fly.

He got the cat all right, but he got the McCanns' window as well, for the stone skipped off the wall right into the middle of it. There was a big star of splits right across the pane.

"The window!" Miss McCann cried.

"Skewball!" yelled Nessie, never giving a damn about the window, so long as her cat was in one piece, unexploded.

The cat leapt off the wall as though the hounds of death were after it.

But it didn't run towards us. It ran the other

way, through the hedge into the front of the Nearys' house, where it cowered.

The big policeman came up to the young policeman who had chucked the stone.

"That was damned bright!" he said, indicating the broken window.

Then another stone came out of the back of the crowd.

It hit the big policeman on the leg.

Suddenly a whole pack of cops were headed for us, leaping out of the backs of the tenders, pelting down the street and under the tape to get the stone chucker.

"Time we were out of this, Brian," said Val nervously. But she couldn't get the chair moved, because people were crowding all around us. Somebody went belting off down the street, but we weren't able to see who it was.

"What about the cat?" Nessie demanded, holding her ground, or trying to, as the police forced the crowd back.

"Your man bust our window!" Miss McCann shouted indignantly.

"The cops is running mad!" somebody else yelled.

Then the police collared somebody. It was Conrad Taylor. Three policemen grabbed him, and the next minute they had him off his feet, running for the back of the tender, with his legs trailing along the road as he kicked and clawed at them.

Then the stones started really flying.

"Fight! Fight!" somebody shouted, but I didn't get seeing the fight, because Val had had enough. She scarpered up the street the only way we could go, weaving in and out among the crowd, squeaky front wheel and all. As we headed for the Road, a whole crowd from the flats were running into battle with milk bottles and stuff, ready to have a go at the police. Old Malcolmson was somewhere at the back, bawling orders at everyone to stop, and nobody was paying a blind bit of heed to him. It was sad to see him lost in the middle of the rumpus like that, waving his arms to make them stop and being ignored.

"Where are we going?" I said.

"We're going to my house," she said. "There's no getting through there to your place."

She was probably right and anyway, I had no choice in the matter. I have to go where I'm pushed.

"Valerie!" Val's mum said, when Val came in through the front gate.

"Oh, Mummy!" Val said. Val was really upset. She was pale and puffed, and kind of wild-eyed with all the excitement.

"There's trouble down the Road, Mummy," Val said. "Brian and I were caught in it."

Val blinked down at her mum. Mrs Martin isn't very big. It seemed odd to have Val mummy-ing her from on high. Val must get her height from her dad.

"You did the right thing bringing poor Brian up

here out of it," said Mrs Martin. "Your father's just left the house this minute, on his way to see what he can do."

I wasn't too happy about the "poor Brian" bit.

"They were stoning the police, Mum!" Val said.

"I hear the police started it," said Mrs Martin, and she bustled us into the house.

She had visitors, and not the kind I would have been expecting to see in Pastor Martin's house ... Mrs Neary and Teresa were there, sitting at the table drinking mugs of tea.

"You know my daughter Valerie, Mrs Neary?" Val's mum said. "And Brian. You'll know Brian Hanna. He lives down near you."

"Hullo," Teresa said.

Mrs Neary didn't say anything. She looked as if she might have been crying.

The vibes weren't good.

"I've sent for Father Lewis, Mrs Neary," said Val's mum. "He'll be coming down to pick you up."

"You're a Christian woman, Mrs Martin," said Mrs Neary.

"It's the least we could do," said Val's mum. "Mr Malcolmson was right to bring you here."

"*Him!*" said Teresa, and she looked as if she was going to say something else, but she didn't.

"You were as well away from there, dear," said Val's mum, then she remembered us.

"Perhaps you would take Brian out to the back, Valerie," she said. I noticed that she didn't suggest that Teresa should go with us. Teresa is about fifteen. She has long black hair and a pale face, and she was holding on to her mum's hand, tightly. She didn't look as if she was in any mood to play games.

"Yes, all right," Val said.

As we were going out of the kitchen door I heard Val's mum say: "Do you know, Mrs Neary, I think the best thing would be for us all to say a prayer, right here and now, to the good Lord."

I bet that went down a basinful!

We went out, but not into the back. We went into the garden.

"I don't know why we have to have them in our house," Val said, meaning the Nearys. She was over the shock of finding Catholics on the doormat and heading for ground she felt mentally at home on.

"Mr Malcolmson brought them, doing his Good Samaritan as usual," I said. "There'll have been the usual panic, and I don't suppose they'd have fancied standing round in a crowd with the neighbours, considering it must have been some of the neighbours who *did* the job."

"You don't know that," Val said.

"I know the Young Defenders," I said.

Val looked as if she was about to protest, but then she didn't. Even she couldn't find a reason why it *wouldn't* be them.

"It's the usual get-the-Catholics-out-of-our-streets job," I said.

"You'd think they'd have some of their own kind they could turn to," Val said indignantly.

"Most of their own kind have already gone," I said.

"If the Nearys had any wit they'd have cleared off too," she said. "They brought this trouble on themselves."

"The Nearys have lived in Cleaver Street for years," I said. "They used to get on all right with everybody, before the trouble."

"There was bound to be trouble," she said. "Their sort always bring it."

"I don't think Sean Neary is an IRA man," I said. "Do you?"

"For all I know, he is!" Val said, determined not to lose ground in her argument.

"Of course he's not," I said. "You know fine well he's not. He's a Holy Mary Catholic, up the road to Mass every time he gets the chance, but that doesn't make him an IRA man."

"How 'of course'?" she burst out. "It's a Protestant street, and Sean Neary is a Catholic. There is no call for anyone to be living in a street they don't belong in, and maybe going off and telling tales to people that want to know things, on a Sunday morning when they are in their churches."

"So he's a spy for the IRA?" I said.

"I don't know if he is or isn't," she said. "That's not the point. There are some he knows who will be, and they'll talk to him *because of* where he lives, and they'll find out things."

"What's there to find out?" I said.

"Mr Leadbetter's brother got shot," she said. "Answering his own door in his own street. Somebody had to point out what door to knock on, hadn't they? That's all I'm saying. It would be a whole lot better if Catholics like the Nearys stuck to their own areas, but they didn't, and now they are getting their comeuppance."

She was fierce about it. I was beginning to get annoyed as well.

"'*I wouldn't have one about the place!*'" I said. It was daft, trying to blame Stan's brother's murder on the Nearys, just because they were Catholics.

"Right!" she said.

She thought I was agreeing with her. She didn't get the reference. It was Lord Brookeborough who said that, our one-time Prime Minister of the Protestant-Parliament-for-a-Protestant-people at Stormont. What he meant was what *she* meant. Any Catholic is a potential informer, a potential enemy of the State, a weakness that other Catholics, the terrorists, the IRA and whatnot, can use if they want to. The English picked up the remark, years after it was made, and there was a whole fuss about it. Any Prime Minister should have the wit not to say a thing like that about a third of the population he's supposed to be representing. Fifty years of thinking like that, and treating Catholics accordingly, bred the mess we are in.

"If you have no trust in people, then you can't expect them to trust you," I said.

60

"I don't trust them," said Val. "I don't trust any Catholic. Catholics have killed and hurt too many people that I am fond of. Catholics are all the same underneath. You should know that better than anyone."

"Yes," I said.

Then she realized what she had just said.

"Oh," she said. "Oh."

"It's OK," I said. "I don't mind."

"Yes, you do," she said. "Of course you do."

"I was in my bloody pram," I said. "I didn't *know*, did I?"

"I should never have said that to you," she said.

Well, maybe she was right, she shouldn't have said it to me, of all people. I suppose she thought I would start sobbing, or something, but you don't. I don't. OK. My mum, my dad. They went shopping. They left me in the pram outside, and there was an IRA bomb in the shop.

That's how I got my wonky legs, and my chair.

It's how I lost my mum and dad.

My Auntie Mae's always telling me about how well my mum cleaned up, when they dug her out of the rubble.

She was like a princess in her coffin, so I'm told.

My dad was a bit more difficult. They kept the coffin lid down on him. There are some of them that you have to, because the bits they scrape off the walls don't add up to something that is recognizably a person.

That's why I should have it in for the IRA and

61

the Catholics, that and my legs.

I don't properly remember them, my mum and dad. Just their photos on the wall in my room, where Auntie Mae hung them up.

I ought to hate the Catholics, but it *wasn't them*. They didn't do it. The people who planted the bomb were Catholics, probably, definitely the IRA, because they claimed it. That isn't what I mean. There's a spirit in the air here, a hate and distrust all around us, a trap. My Auntie Mae dinned that into me, as soon as I was old enough to understand. She says that if you start hating, you're in it, caught like everybody else. The only way to avoid the trap is not to do that.

So I don't hate Catholics, and I don't hate my own people. I just wish things were different.

"Brian?" Val said. "Brian, I'm really sorry, Brian. I didn't mean to hurt you."

Then ...

B-O-O-M!

"That's the Nearys' house blown up," I said.

"Oh, Brian!" she said, and she started to shake.

CHAPTER SEVEN

The boom wasn't the Nearys' house going up in smoke. It was the piece of pipe some of their neighbours had left on the window-sill, as a get-out message. Making something look like a bomb isn't difficult, if you have the type of mind that wants to do that sort of thing. The army came to take a look at it, and decided not to take any risks, so they blew it up with one of their robots. As a necessary side effect, most of the windows in the houses round it were blown in as well, but I doubt if that bothered the Young Defenders from the flats.

We didn't know the result until Sean Neary came with the priest, Father Lewis, and Mr Malcolmson, who was still flustered but very much the sergeant major, taking control. Sean Neary had a suitcase full of things that he had rescued from the house.

Everybody had come out into the Martins' garden, after the boom, and it was Teresa Neary who spotted them coming.

"Here's Daddy!" Teresa said, and she left her mother and went down to the gate.

Mrs Neary didn't move. She stood beside Val's mum, a little crumpled woman, her hand against her mouth, biting her wedding ring.

Father Lewis went straight to her, and Sean Neary took hold of Teresa.

That left Mr Malcolmson looking as if he thought he should be somewhere else. He went up to Val's mum.

"Is the pastor not back yet?" he said.

Val's mum shook her head.

"Things are very nasty down there, missus," Mr Malcolmson said. "You'd do well to advise these people to stay out of it."

"Out?" said Mrs Neary sharply.

"Now, Eileen..." said Father Lewis, catching hold of her arm.

"Oh, I'm all right, Father," said Mrs Neary.

"There's two policemen in hospital," said Mr Malcolmson. "They went after the lads in a tender, and somebody chucked a milk bottle filled with petrol into the back. Now the police have the street cordoned off, and they're doing house to house."

It was really odd, thinking about it. There we all were in the big garden in front of Pastor Martin's house: Mrs Martin the pastor's wife, the parish priest, Mr Malcolmson, Val and me and the Nearys, a real oddball collection. We were standing around in the sun on the sort of day when you'd have been saying to yourself what a nice summer it was turning out to be ... and down the Road, at our street, and Cleaver Street, and the flats, and round the mission, there was hell to pay with the army blowing things up and people chucking petrol bombs at the police and houses getting searched.

All over nothing, was what I thought, but the signal in Val's eyes was still, *All over the Nearys*.

Maybe she was right, in a horrible way. If they had upped and moved out years ago when the troubles got going, it would never have happened.

Sean Neary went to Mrs Neary, and took her away from the priest. She held on to her husband. She had gone shivery.

"Perhaps I should go down there..." the priest said uneasily.

"I don't think that would be a good idea at all," said Val's mum quickly.

"You'd get your head in your hands," said Mr Malcolmson. He avoided Father Lewis's eye when he said it, but there was a kind of glee in his voice. I couldn't figure him out. I was left thinking that anywhere else he'd have been quite a good person, involved, trying to help the neighbours, running a youth club or something. Here, it was the Young Defenders band and all the poison that went with it.

"We'll have to get our things out," said Sean Neary, over Mrs Neary's shoulder. She had collapsed into him. Her face was buried in his chest.

"It might be more sensible to leave that to me," said Mr Malcolmson.

"You?" said Teresa Neary, in a voice of disbelief.

"That's very good of you, Mr Malcolmson," said Val's mum.

"I'll do what I can to get your stuff moved, Mr Neary," said Mr Malcolmson. "If I can. I'm sure I don't have to explain the problem to you."

"Who cares about the stuff?" Mrs Neary pulled her head back, and looked at us defiantly. "What does it matter about any old things, so long as we are well out of it?"

"It's our stuff, damn it!" said Sean Neary.

"It's your skin you should be looking out for, Mr Neary," said Mr Malcolmson. "If you take my advice you'll not show your nose in Cleaver Street again."

"I think you should pay heed to Mr Malcolmson, Mr Neary," said Val's mum.

"I'd say that was sound, Sean," said Father Lewis. I didn't take to him. He was old, and lost-looking.

"Mr Malcolmson will move what he can for you," said Val's mum, stepping up the power. "I'm sure that my husband will be able to calm things down enough for you to get a van load out, later. But it really would be very foolish to go down there and start shifting things now, with the police running about."

"I can't go down there *without* the police running about," said Sean Neary. "And they're not going to sit there all day guarding the house, with no one in it."

"I don't give a damn about the house, Sean!" said Mrs Neary, and she started crying.

"Now, now, Eileen..." said Father Lewis, making vague moves towards her, and backing off again.

"Come back in the house, Mrs Neary," said Val's mum, taking charge as usual, and she took hold of Mrs Neary's arm and drew her back towards the house. They were a kind of crab-group, going towards the door, with Sean Neary and Mrs Martin supporting Mrs Neary, and the priest coming up behind.

Teresa went up to Mr Malcolmson.

"You're the man that runs that band, aren't you?" she said.

"Yes," said Mr Malcolmson.

"Then you know who did this to us and you ought to tell the police," Teresa said. Her hands were shaking, clenched by her sides.

"It was your ones did it!" she said, almost spitting the words at him.

Mr Malcolmson looked at her. Then he looked away at me, and he winked. It was very nasty the way he did it, including me in like that.

"You ... you *bastard!*" said Teresa, and then she walked away from us, heading towards the house. Halfway down the path she turned back and shouted, "You're a pack of Orange bastards! I hope the Provies get you and your bastard band!"

"There's the thanks you get!" said Mr Malcolmson.

He meant it too. He thought she *should* have been thanking him. He sounded hurt.

Val didn't say anything. She had gone very pale. She loitered beside us, blinking distress signals over my head.

"Well, young Hanna," said Mr Malcolmson. "Are you coming back down the road to pick up the pieces?"

"I'll go with you," said Val.

"Indeed you will not, young lady!" said Mr Malcolmson. "Pastor Martin would flay me alive if I took you back there, and that's a fact."

"He's right, Val," I said. "You stay here."

"Help your mother," said Mr Malcolmson. "She has enough on her hands, with Mrs Neary throwing up all over the carpet indoors."

Val hesitated, but she went off. She isn't used to disobeying orders.

Mr Malcolmson wheeled me down Val's road.

"Will you be able to get the stuff out of Neary's house, Mr Malcolmson?" I asked him.

"Oh yes, sure," he said. "Nobody will go near it now."

"Won't they?"

"I'll have one or two of the lads keep an eye on things," he said. "We don't want the house damaged. It didn't belong to them. It was only rented. They're grand wee homes, Cleaver Street houses. We wouldn't want anybody squatting there, or the like of that. It will need to go to decent people. That will all have to be arranged."

"Protestants, you mean?" I said. I knew it was what he meant, but I wanted to hear him say it.

"That was the object of the operation, son!" he said cheerfully. "Mission, you might say, accomplished!"

We crossed over the Road, and turned into the streets.

It was all quiet. Not a policeman in sight.

"They're grand streets," Mr Malcolmson said. "It's a grand place to live. I wouldn't swap it for anywhere else."

He meant that as well. His streets, his people. His military manner hid a confusion between his idea of himself and what must have been a half comprehension that he was being used by Stan and the UDA. Maybe he couldn't see it, I don't really know.

We didn't go down Cleaver Street, because there was still broken glass and rubble and stuff on the road. People were busy sticking hardboard up on the windows. The army's controlled explosion had taken the window-frame out of the Nearys' front. Mrs Neary's blue curtains were blowing in the breeze. There was a police tender at the end of the street, but no policemen in sight, although I suppose there must have been policemen in it. There was no sign of the tender that got the petrol bomb.

Ollie Leadbetter was standing at the corner of our street.

"The air smells a bit better round here with that day's work done, Mr Malcolmson," said Ollie.

"Aye, it does," said Mr Malcolmson.

"My da said to tell you Conrad Taylor got beat up," said Ollie.

"I was there," said Mr Malcolmson.

"My da said that the UDA would be looking into it, and you're to tell Mrs Taylor they'll be round to see her," said Ollie. He went off.

Conrad Taylor's daddy is inside. He's doing time for slitting a wee barman's throat. The Loyalist Prisoners' Aid takes Mrs Taylor to see him in their minibus, visiting days, and they see she is all right, because it was a Political. There can't be that much that is political about sticking a knife in a Catholic barman, but that is the way they see it. Apparently Conrad's daddy was in a UVF active service unit, and they had the barman on their list.

Maybe Sean Neary got off lightly after all.

"Everything is hunky-dory here then, Hanna," said Mr Malcolmson, dumping me at my door.

He went off to see to things, our street organizer. He would make sure the Nearys' house wasn't looted. He'd see to getting the McCanns' window fixed. He would read his Young Defenders a lecture in the band rooms at their next meeting, and he'd go to bed with his self-esteem reasserted.

I had to let myself in, because Auntie Mae wasn't back from work yet, and Billy hadn't showed up either. It was a good thing I had my key with me in the chair bag.

I went and sat in our back kitchen, waiting for the kettle to boil, and wondering what it would be like to be the Nearys. I wondered if I would have the guts to sit it out the way they had, with one Catholic family after another moving away from the streets around them, as the process of dividing the town up into tribal zones gathered momentum. Really it would have been much easier for them to clear out. Val was right, in that way.

Imagine sitting there, year in, year out, always expecting something to happen, with the only certainty being that one day it will. There are Protestant and Catholic families doing that all over Northern Ireland, sitting in houses in the "wrong" streets, or in the "wrong" townlands, waiting.

The Nearys should have left Cleaver Street. It would have been the *wrong* thing to do, if you believe in heroics and setting a community example, and not letting yourself be bullied into anything ... but it was surely the *right* thing to do if you were a man with a family and wanted a life for them that wasn't hemmed in by fear of the next knock on the door.

If it had been *us* – me, and Auntie Mae, and Billy – Billy wouldn't have wanted to go. I could imagine him sitting it out there, waiting, refusing to let any Catholic drive him out. Just like the Nearys. What we have we hold. No surrender.

That's what the *bam-bam-bam* of the drums says. It is a beat of fear, but the fear is in the drummer.

Every Twelfth of July our people, the Protestant Orangemen, are out in their thousands, parading behind the drums. The *bam-bam-bam* is to frighten the Catholics, but it goes deeper than that. We make a big noise to scare the bogeyman, like a child shouting for fear of the dark.

Bam-bam-bam.

I wish I knew how to still the drums. The drumming and the marching goes on and on and on. Even when the drum beat dies, it stays there in your head.

Billy used to take Hicky and me out with him on the Twelfth, until I told Auntie Mae that I didn't want to go any more. She told him some half-lie to get me out of it. But not going didn't mean I escaped. You can hear the *bam-bam-bam* for miles around the town, in the sunny summer air.

I remember sitting in our back with Auntie Mae and listening to it.

She started talking about my mum and my dad.

She said it need never have happened, if it hadn't been for going-for-the-new-curtains.

Then she started crying.

She said it was the drums getting at her.

"You're not to be one of *those*, Brian," she said. "You're not to be one of *those*."

"Uncle Billy is," I said.

"He doesn't know any better," she said, and there was a sudden fierceness about it that took me aback.

"He's a good man, your Uncle Billy," she said.

"He thinks he's doing what he has to do. He thinks there's no other way."

Then she got out her baking tin and she made me a jam sponge and we had it for our tea, and saved a bit for Billy when he came home, so he could have it when he was watching the late night rerun of the Twelfth Day Processions on TV.

CHAPTER EIGHT

There was a big stir in the street, round about half-past seven.

Stan Leadbetter turned up accompanied by Councillor Paden, our local representative of the kick-the-Pope brigade: political division. They all trooped into Mr Malcolmson's house, for a council of war.

Then Mr Malcolmson came out, and went off to the flats to talk to Conrad Taylor's mum and Conrad's Uncle Alexander, who was with him when Conrad got lifted.

Then he came back and he and Stan and Councillor Paden came to our house.

"Mae? Billy?" said Stan, and he eased himself into my Auntie Mae's armchair. Auntie Mae went out of the room without speaking. Stan never blinked an eyelid. She didn't count at all, as far as he was concerned. I wondered if the others counted either in the final analysis. I knew I didn't and Mr Malcolmson certainly didn't. Billy didn't count either. I wasn't sure about the councillor, who had resources of his own.

"I've seen you on TV," Billy said, shaking Councillor Paden's hand.

"Is this the young rip?" Councillor Paden said, turning to me. He was younger than he looked on TV, and very smart and snazzy in his suit and Ulster tie.

"The councillor wants a word with you, young fella," Stan said, relaxing back in the chair.

Stan beamed at Councillor Paden and Billy and me, in turn. We were all big men together, having a conference. Mr Malcolmson was stiff in his seat – on parade before the big brass.

Warning lights and bells started ringing in my head. There'd been a row in the street, arising from the stone throwing. And I was the one who suggested stone throwing...

It looked like I was for the high jump.

"It wasn't my fault," I said quickly. "It was all down to Miss McCann's cat."

"Don't get excited, son," Stan said. "We're not here to blame anybody, just to get the record straight." He winked at Billy. You would have thought we were being visited by royalty from the way Billy lapped it up.

"Well, Brian," said Councillor Paden. "We'll have a wee talk."

"Yes," I said. I don't know how he knew my name. Well, I did know, once I thought about it.

Stan would have briefed him. It was interesting, because everybody knows that Stan is the local paramilitary commander, and Councillor Paden is not supposed to have any connection with the paramilitaries, but there you are. I suppose that Stan was there in his role as Community Leader and Keeper of the Peace, at least that is the way the councillor would have put it if anybody had asked him.

I didn't like Paden any more than I liked the paramilitaries, that was my thought. And I wasn't going to admit anything about starting the stone throwing, in case they decided to make me a scapegoat.

"Stanley has given me a general picture of the trouble you have been having round here recently with the Security Forces, Brian," Councillor Paden said, leaning forward to speak to me, as though I might have to lip read or something, because I'm in a wheelchair. "But I'd like to hear your own version of the story."

"What bit?" I said cautiously. Malcolmson might have told them it was my suggestion to chuck the stones. Well, it was. There was nothing wrong with that. How was I to know it would start a riot?

"You were with a crowd of neighbours and bystanders at the end of Cleaver Street when the police ran into the crowd and severely beat young Conrad Taylor," the councillor said. "Isn't that right?"

"Yes," I said.

End of problem.

It was Conrad getting beaten up they were on about, not who suggested chucking stones! I should have realized it would be. Conrad getting beaten up by the police is the sort of story Councillor Paden has made a career from.

"You were in the crowd, in your chair?"

"Yes."

"The lad is supposed to be getting a new one," Mr Malcolmson put in. "The social services said he would get one, but it is a long time coming."

It was the only time he spoke. He sat back looking satisfied at his intervention on my behalf and nodded at me.

"I'll make a note of that," the councillor said gravely, and he wrote it down. Billy started giving dates, but the councillor cut him off. "Just drop the details into my advice centre," he said.

"Right!" said Billy, and he beamed at me and Mr Malcolmson.

"Well, Brian," said the councillor. "You were there in the crowd, with your wheelchair, when the police started laying about them. Is that right?"

"The police were trying to keep the crowd back from the bomb," I said.

"One of the policemen shattered the window of a house with a stone, and the crowd reacted strongly," said the councillor. "A missile of some sort came out of the crowd and struck one of the policemen?"

"Yes," I said.

"Did you see the young man, Taylor, throw anything at the police?"

"No," I said. "I didn't see Conrad Taylor until the cops got him."

"And Conrad's uncle is prepared to swear that Conrad was walking down the street, on his way back to the flats, minding his own business, and not involved in the row with the police at all. Conrad didn't even witness the window being broken in the first place," Stan said.

"I don't see how the police could have known who chucked the stone," I said. "It came out of the back of the crowd."

The councillor smiled, and nodded.

"You didn't see Taylor throw the stone, and you never saw him with a stone in his hand?"

Never is a long time. I've seen Conrad Taylor chuck a few bricks in his time, but I knew that wasn't what he meant. "No," I said.

There's no love lost between Conrad Taylor and me, but I wasn't going to get him into trouble … anyway, it was the truth.

"I think the police wanted to arrest somebody," I said. "I don't think Conrad had anything to do with the stone."

"But you saw the police manhandle him?" the councillor persisted.

"They dragged Conrad through the crowd," I said. "He was kicking and screeching. They were giving him a beating." Then I had a bad thought.

"I won't have to go to court or anything on this, will I?" I said.

"Never worry about that, Brian," said Stan, which didn't do a lot to reassure me.

"I wouldn't want to go to court," I said.

I wasn't feeling proud of myself when I said it. I didn't want them using me, the way they use everybody else.

"Look, son," said the councillor, in his special voice for calming cripples. "What we are trying to show is that the police and the army in this area have developed a pattern of response to minor incidents, designed to *provoke* situations where they can walk in, take the place over, and generally act the big lad. It isn't accidental. This is coming down from the very top, the Prime Minister in Downing Street, and the intention is to put the Protestant people in the bottom place, and show them the Brits are the bosses."

"Right!" Big Stan said.

"Two separate incidents in twenty-four hours," said the councillor. "First the search of the band rooms attached to the mission, on almost no pretext at all, and then, when that didn't turn anything up, this business. It's an excuse to come in here and look around for anything they can find, on the grounds that lawless elements have attacked the police. We've all heard that before."

"The police have to learn to keep in line, just like anybody else," said Stan.

"Did any of the police strike you, son?" Councillor

Paden said, turning back to me.

"No," I said.

"But you were frightened by the aggressive attitude of the police towards the crowd?"

"After the stones," I said. "Yes. I was afraid because I can't get out of crowds easily in my chair. I can't afford to get caught in a riot."

"His friends rescued him from being trampled on, Councillor," Billy put in.

"It was Val," I said.

"Val?" Councillor Paden asked.

"I don't think you need bother about her, Councillor," Stan said, and he leant forward and whispered something in the councillor's ear.

"We'll keep out of that water!" the councillor said, with a grin.

"I doubt the pastor might not be too pleased!" said Stan.

"Well, I think we have all we need," the councillor said, and he stood up.

He patted me on the head. You'd think I was a little dog. The head patters are definitely the worst ones.

He dropped a pound coin into my lap, as if I had no hands.

"Thanks," I said, not very enthusiastically. I suppose he thought I could buy myself a bag of sweets.

"Keep up the exercises, Brian," the councillor said.

"What exercises?" I asked Billy, when he came

back from seeing them out the door.

"He thinks you are doing exercises for your legs, because you go to the Joy Club," Billy said.

"My legs are useless," I said.

Then the neighbours started coming in. They were all on about how great I was, and what a good man Councillor Paden was, and how he would sort out the army and the police so that they wouldn't come harassing us any more.

"Councillor Paden's not like some," Billy said. "He's going to see about Brian's chair."

Everybody beamed at me.

I let them.

I was glad to be out of it, unscathed.

Stan Leadbetter gets to me that way. It isn't what he does, the Community Leader bit, the social welfare and all that stuff. It's what lies behind it. The Community Leader bit is a front, nothing more and nothing less.

The paramilitaries, both sides, have their own system of law and order, paying a kind of lip service to the prevailing morality ... you get beaten up if you fool around with someone else's wife, and you get a breeze block dropped on your leg if you go raiding sweetie shops.

The system's real importance is that it estab-lishes the paramilitaries' position.

I got myself out of the crowd, and wheeled into Auntie Mae, in the back.

"Well?" she said, not one bit pleased.

"They're trying to get Conrad Taylor off the

hook," I said. "That's what they wanted to speak to me about."

"Don't get mixed up with them, Brian," she said. "Any of them. Promise me? If you get mixed up with them too, it would finish me."

"I know," I said.

"I don't want you changing on me like Billy," she said.

She was as near to despair as I have ever seen her.

"It wasn't like that," I said.

"They'll use you if they can," she said. "They'll use anybody they take a mind to."

"I'm not Billy," I said.

There was a long silence.

"He can't help it, you know," she said. "Billy just goes with the crowd."

"I know," I said.

"It was what happened to you that did for him," she said. "He was never that bitter before. It changed him. He's not the same man since."

"He's not the martyr type," I said.

"He's not a big man at all," she said. She was struggling with the idea that she shouldn't say things to me against Billy, but they were things we both knew already, she had no need to say them.

Sometime, someday, in the wrong place, with people egging him on, Billy might let the bitterness that was put in him by what happened to my mum and dad and me boil over. If that happened, and things went wrong, she would have no Billy left at all, and I don't know if she could live with that.

"You and Billy," she said. "You're all I've got, Brian."

"Nothing's going to happen to Billy," I said, trying to soothe her. "It'll be all right."

I made her a cup of tea.

There didn't seem to be much else I could do.

CHAPTER NINE

Billy bounded into the house the next morning, waving the newsletter.

"You're in the paper, Brian!" he shouted. "We'll all be famous." I don't know what he was all delighted for. I could have curled up.

At least I didn't make the front page. The IRA had killed a man and his eldest son in a farmhouse in Fermanagh. They'd shot them in a field by the house, with the man's wife looking on. The IRA specialise in eldest sons in Fermanagh, it's a way of trying to nudge the settlers off their farms. The newsletter had it splashed across the front page. Councillor Paden's bit about the harassment of a Loyalist area in our town had been relegated to an inside page, and the biggest thing about it was the picture of the councillor and the two Miss McCanns with their broken window.

"The RUC won't get away with it this time!" Billy said. "Police harassment."

My Auntie Mae took one look at the paper, and one look at me, and then she went and put her hat and coat on.

I wheelied after her into the hall.

"I didn't know it was going to get in the paper," I said.

"It's not your fault, Brian," she said. "I just don't want you mixed up in things like that."

"I am mixed up in it," I said.

"Only because you are here," she said.

"I am here."

"Sometimes I blame myself for that," she said. "I should have taken you away out of this, to some other place."

She used to go on about getting Billy to up hooks and go to live in England, Sheffield or some place, for my sake. She was always afraid I would be dragged into things, because of what happened to my mum and dad.

"I like it here," I said, lying in my teeth.

"Do you?" she said.

She let the words sit between us.

"Most of the time," I said.

"I wouldn't be here but for Billy," she said.

She went out of the door on that note, and banged past Duggie who was on the way up our path, without so much as looking at him.

"What's the matter with your auntie?" he said, giving me a puzzled look.

"She's not herself this morning," I said lamely.

"Your uncle is one pleased man," said Duggie.

"He's shown the paper right round the street."

"And why wouldn't I?" Billy said, bobbing out of the kitchen at us.

"Great man yourself!" said Duggie. "It is time the RUC quit harassing us, and went where the action is."

"We could have done with a few more of them in Fermanagh last night!" Billy said, looking at the blood-soaked pictures on the front page.

"The IRA need teaching a lesson!" Duggie said. "It's about time the government let the police loose to do it."

"There'd have been no holding back when we had our own parliament," Billy said. "They are murderers the whole pack of them, from Maggie Thatcher down. If she lets the IRA come over the border and shoot decent Protestants like that, then she has blood on her hands, and all the shilly-shallying dances she does with Dublin won't wash it off her."

There was nothing I could say. A Protestant farmer and his son shot dead in a field their family had worked for generations. The eldest son … always the eldest son. More widows, more tears, more country funerals, and every drip of blood on those fields counted as one more score against the Catholics, *all* the Catholics, not just the mad bad ones. I couldn't blame Billy for seeing it that way, against the drums and their message. Protestant fields were the same as Protestant streets, the bits and pieces which went to make up his life were under siege. Those distant deaths, in Fermanagh, the two of them, father and son, were only the echo of the deaths he'd seen all around him.

Those deaths, like every other murder we've been through, stitched Billy's colours ever more firmly to the mast. No surrender! If they took away his fields, his streets, his flags and bunting, poor Billy would be left with nowhere to go. I didn't agree with him, but I knew what he was at and I couldn't see how to change things for him, so that there was no need to fight, when every turn things took seemed to drive him to it.

And Duggie, and Hicky, and Ollie Leadbetter, and Mr Malcolmson. All of them ... even Stan Leadbetter had followed behind his brother's coffin to the grave. It was no wonder they turned the way they did. The fear was in them that they would be let down by the British, betrayed into Popery, and a Papish Republic ... unless they took a stand. So they *take* a stand, and for all the crude gutter violence of it, that stand has a kind of beauty, if you see beauty that way. The Protestant version is as valid as the other sort, though it lacks a poet to say the words.

"It's all bad," I said.

"It's murder!" Billy said. "Murdering bastard Fenians!"

"Yes," I said.

"They'll pay," he said. "They'll pay double for every drop of Protestant blood that's spilt!"

"You're right there," Duggie said.

Billy was all hyped up. I was glad to see the back of him by the time he went off, but worried too. My worry was for Auntie Mae, as well as him. If Billy got hurt or killed or jailed because of what he believed in, the fact that she didn't believe it would seem like a betrayal to her, even if she was right, and he was wrong.

I lolled around outside the house with Duggie, busy not listening to him, worrying about Billy, worrying about Auntie Mae, worrying about me, worrying about Hicky, and worrying about where all this worrying was going to get me.

It hadn't got me very far, when one of the worries came rolling up.

It was Hicky, strolling down the pavement, bold as brass and evidently un-arrested.

"I thought the police had you lifted," I said, because the police had been lifting almost everybody else, in their follow-up operations, and it seemed natural that Hicky would have gone as well.

"Oh, I got lifted all right," Hicky said.

"What for?" I asked.

Hicky didn't answer that. He said, "I can handle the cops, you know," and left it at that. He had his being-crafty face on. I don't know how he handles the cops, because he can't handle anybody else.

"Hanna is in the paper," Duggie said, and he showed Hicky the piece about me.

"B-R-I-A-N H-A-N-N-A," Duggie said, picking out the letters for Hicky, just to prove it was me.

"Yeah?" said Hicky. "What does it say?"

That is one thing about Hicky and not being able to read properly. He knows we know, and he doesn't try to make out otherwise like some of them do – and end up going into the Ladies' instead of the Gents'.

Duggie read it all out to him, and I sat there thinking they'd used me all right, because what was in the paper had happened, but it hadn't happened the way the councillor made it sound.

"They'll be saying the cops planted the bomb themselves next," I said. "Just to get a chance to do a good search round the houses."

"Maybe they did!" Duggie said.

"The police don't plant bombs," I said.

"It wasn't a bomb," said Duggie. "It was a *fake* one. And it gave them a damn good excuse."

"You don't mean that," I said.

"It might have been the soldiers," said Hicky, sticking his oar in.

"Yeah," said Duggie. "Why not?"

I gave up.

"Maybe the Nearys did it themselves," I said. "They wanted to make it look as if the Protestants chased them out, so they could get priority housing in a Catholic area."

"Yeah, yeah!" said Hicky.

"I bet that was it," said Duggie.

"The police probably put them up to it," I said.

"Yeah!" said Hicky.

"Or the CIA," I said, keeping a straight face.

Duggie caught on at last.

"Yeah!" he said. "James Bond. Bang! Bang! Bang!"

"Where does James Bond come into it?" Hicky asked.

"It's a good thing you are a special case, Hanna," said Duggie. "Some of the things you say would get you into trouble round here, if you weren't in your wheelchair."

He wasn't too pleased at having his leg pulled, and I wasn't very proud of myself for doing it. Baiting people doesn't help. I was out to help him, not hurt him.

"You might get on television, Hanna," Hicky said. He was still staring at the paper which Duggie had handed to him, as if he was reading it.

"What for?" I said.

"Because you are a handicap, and the cops might have killed you," Hicky said.

"He'd take some killing, old Hanna!" Duggie said.

"I've already survived one bomb," I said, thinking *but my mum and dad didn't*. They got their photos in the paper. Eight people were killed in the explosion. I don't know who the other six were. I don't really know anything about it. I've never even been back where it was. It wasn't down town, it was the shopping centre. My mum and dad were just married. They were in love. They were young. My mum was a trainee hairdresser and my dad was training to be a teacher, and then my mum got pregnant and they got married and had me, all in a rush. The next thing was they got the new house and they went shopping to get curtains. My Auntie Mae says they wanted new red curtains, because it was a new house, and my mum had been saving up all their money for the deposit on the curtains. They wheeled me down to the shopping centre. They left the pram outside and they went in. I don't know whether they ever had time to pick the curtains, or sign the HP agreement.

I don't care about the bloody curtains.

I just wish I could remember what my mum and dad were like.

Auntie Mae and Billy had to fight to get me. The social services woman told them their house wasn't suitable and there was a big row about it, but my Auntie Mae was determined and Billy backed her up. In the end the social services let me go home to them when I got out of hospital, after all the operations on my spine, and that is why I am where I am, and I am what I am.

"You're not to hate anybody, little Brian," my Auntie Mae drummed into me when I was really tiny. "It was God's will took your legs away, and your mammy and daddy."

I think that maybe backfired, on God! Anyway, Auntie Mae saved me from what I might have turned to in the circumstances, and left me not particularly anxious to be the star of a TV interview about how the police were roughing up good Protestants.

Hicky and Duggie were excited about it.

They hung around in the street all morning in case the television people came to follow up the story in the paper, but mercifully nobody did. I was browned off, but puzzled as well. All the usual cowboys were hanging about the street, Ollie Leadbetter and French and that lot – French had a black eye from somewhere – and there was a lot of nudge and wink stuff going on.

CHAPTER TEN

I was still wondering what was behind all the nudge and wink when Val came round in the afternoon to give me a push. We went up the park.

"Do you know anything I don't know about what's going on round here today?" I said.

"What do you mean?" she said, blinking down at me from on high.

"They're all very pleased with themselves," I said.

"Well, I suppose the police have egg on their faces," she said. "They set out to find something, and they didn't. It makes them look silly. Particularly when they do it by busting their way into our mission hall."

"They didn't bust into the mission hall," I said. "Just the band rooms."

"It's still God's house," she said.

"Yeah," I said. "So it is."

I had a momentary flashback, to Billy and his

van parked outside the mission hall, just *before* the bomb was found at Neary's. Billy, with his van, on a mission for Big Stan and the UDA. *And* his van. What did they want his van for?

That line of thought led on to all sorts of questions, like how convenient a riot can be, if it happens to draw all the cops in the neighbourhood towards it, when you need space to move something you are hiding to a new hiding place.

If that particular thought had legs, then it would explain the general air of smirkyness, of putting-one-over-on-the-cops that I felt around the street. It's not the sort of thing they'd talk to me about.

"Brian?" Val said, taking off her glasses and rubbing them, before slipping them into her pocket.

"Yes?" I said.

"Do you mind if I leave you here a wee minute, Brian? There's somebody down there I want to have a word with."

"OK," I said.

We were on a hill in the park, near the tennis courts. She went running down it, her clumpy shoes making her clumsy.

Two guys were playing tennis.

When they saw her, one of them called a stop.

She went up and talked to him, while the other one went and hit practise shots into the fence.

It was no big surprise.

Once or twice, when she'd been in the park with me, there had been a feeling that we went past the tennis courts more often than we strictly needed to, but still I *was* surprised.

Secret trysts in the park. Pastor and Mrs Martin never let her out over the doorstep without a good reason, and meeting the boyfriend down at the tennis court wouldn't pass as that.

If they knew that she had a boyfriend, they'd go up the wall.

"Hi, stranger," I said, when she came back.

Her pale face was flushed, her eyes glowy, maybe because she hadn't got the specs on.

"You can put your glasses back on now," I said. "The boyfriend is gone."

"*Brian!*" she said.

"Well," I said, teasing her.

She was sitting on the ground, beside my chair. She leant over and plucked a long piece of grass. Then she looked up at me, and stuck it in her mouth, defiantly.

"Val?" I said.

"He's Ronnie Dobbin," she said. "He's in the sixth form at the college."

"That's nice for him," I said. I wouldn't have minded going there myself.

"It's great that you've got somebody," I said. "I'm really pleased, Val."

"Yes," she said. "Me too."

She didn't look at me, but then she did.

"Listen, Brian," she said. "You're not to go telling *anyone* about me and Ronnie, right?"

"If you say so," I said.

95

"Particularly Mummy," she said. "She doesn't like Ronnie."

I let that sink in.

"I don't often meet your mum," I said.

"Don't let anything slip out, if you do," she said. "Mummy knows I come up here, wheeling you. She makes a big deal out of it. If she thought I wasn't wheeling you, I probably wouldn't get out of the house. She's … she's *awkward* about boys, and things like that. So I'm … I'm sort of *using* you, in a way."

"Use on!" I said.

"You're only great, Brian," she said.

We didn't talk a lot, after that.

She wheeled me back to the house.

"You don't mind about Ronnie, do you?" she said, when she was leaving me off.

"Me?" I said. "What have I got to mind about?"

"So long as you don't mind," she said.

She was building up to further revelations, and I thought it would be better to make it easy for her.

"You want to arrange to meet him sometimes," I said. "But your mum won't let you out unless you've got a good copper-bottomed Christian excuse, like wheeling me about in my chair, right? So you want to go and meet Ronnie and let on that you are out with me."

"I couldn't lie to Mummy about it, Brian," she said, sounding very uncomfortable.

"You don't have to lie, exactly," I said. "Do you?"

"I won't," she said.

"I know you won't," I said.

"But you would … you'd help me?" she said.

"Yes," I said. "Yes, of course."

"You're brilliant, Brian Hanna!" she said. "You're a very special person in my life," and off she went.

I sat there in our front room, in my chair. Val was my person. I didn't want to share her with Ronnie, whoever he was. Ronnie with two good legs he could run about and play tennis on... Why did he have to take her from me?

No Val, no Hicky, nobody really except my Auntie Mae, and she's my *auntie*. I could have got upset about it but what was the point? I was building up to snapping myself out of it when the key went in the lock, and in rolled Billy.

I don't know why he wasn't at work, but he wasn't and it was pretty plain he had had a skinful. I made him sit down on the sofa in the kitchen, and got him some coffee, instant and black.

"Billy?" I said.

"Yeah?"

"You know the bomb in Cleaver Street?" I said. "The bomb that wasn't? The thing that was out on the window-sill to scare the Nearys into moving out?"

"Yeah," he said, beginning to sound foxy. He's very bad at being foxy, Billy is. You'd know he wasn't telling you the straight truth just at the moment when he thinks he has the fact hidden deepest.

"That was a diversion," I said. "Wasn't it? To get the cops all up to that end, well away from the mission hall?"

"Naw!" he said. "No way."

"Come on, Billy," I said. "It's me you are talking to."

"Well…" he looked around him in an exaggerated way, as if the Head of MI5 might pop out of the wall. "Well, between you and me, young Brian, yeah! Yeah! Yeah! YEAH!"

"I thought so," I said.

"Then off I tootle in my van like Postman Pat!" he said. "Only you don't know about it, and I never told you, right, Brian?"

Billy laid himself back against the cushions and beamed at me through his glasses triumphantly.

It just about made my day.

I was annoyed with myself over Val – not for what I'd said, but for the way I felt. It was stupid, there was no other name for it … I was annoyed at that, and now on top of it came the realization that Billy was in much deeper than he should have been.

There had been something hidden in the band rooms. I wondered if Mr Malcolmson had known about it, probably not. From Stan Leadbetter's point of view, Mr Malcolmson was small beer, even if he was handy for keeping the lads in check and helping old ladies with their broken windows. He wouldn't *need* to know so *probably* he didn't.

He mightn't have minded anyway.

Stan must have wanted something moved out of the band rooms. I suppose he'd roped Billy into moving it for him. The UDA must have suspected that the band room was still under observation after the first raid, and so Stan had set up an all-hands-to-the-pumps riot, which took the police out of the way long enough to allow Billy to take away whatever had to be got rid of.

I wondered if Billy knew just how dangerous it was. If the police had caught him with stuff in his van, he could have gone to prison for a very long time.

I didn't like to think what that would do to my Auntie Mae.

"You want to be careful, Billy," I said anxiously.

"Oh, I am careful!" he said, rolling his eyes in a knowing way, which served to show how tight he was. He sounded like Hicky, only Hicky grown up. Billy lay there with his legs sprawled off the end of the sofa, balancing his coffee cup on his chest, and boasting about the big operation.

They'd moved the stuff from the back of the mission hall up to somebody's garden.

"There's more than spuds growing up there, Brian, son," he said.

Whatever it was, the stuff, it was six foot under, and wrapped in black plastic.

It would be guns, I suppose. There have to be Loyalist arms caches somewhere, if all the reports of people being arrested shopping for them in

Scotland and Amsterdam are anything to go by. We keep hearing of money being collected and Loyalists being lifted for buying arms and explosives, but the stuff never seems to show up in Northern Ireland. Maybe that's because our side have it down to a fine art, or maybe some of the money that's supposed to go for God and Ulster somehow gets diverted into continental holidays and second cars. I wouldn't know about that. What I did know was that Billy was out of his league when he started mixing with the paramilitaries, and I hoped he knew it.

"Well, I suppose you are all right, so long as the police fell for it," I said.

"The cops got well offside," he said. "The whole thing was A-OK, just the way we planned it. Clockwork."

"There's more than the police has an interest in guns," I said.

"What guns?" he said, doing his foxy bit again.

"Oh, come on," I said. "The Brits could have been on to you."

"We have the Security Forces figured," he said.

"Oh yes?" I said. "What's all this about there being an informer around, then? Or am I just imagining it?"

"I never heard tell of that," Billy said, not looking too pleased.

I was thinking of Val's talk about someone tipping off the Security Forces to search the band rooms.

"We have the whole place taped up," he said, rallying his forces. "Nobody round here would talk to the Brits, or they know what they'd get."

"You know you, Billy?" I said. "You are drunk. That's what you are!"

"Of course I am!" he said happily.

"Just don't go getting drunk in any strange company," I said.

"Meaning?" he said, leaning forward and almost depositing the coffee cup on the floor. I took it from him, because Auntie Mae wouldn't have been pleased at any breakages.

"It is one thing you coming into your own house and telling me about all this," I said. "It might be different, if you were somewhere else."

"Listen, Brian," he said, shaking his head. "You … you know nothing! Understand? *Nothing*."

I nodded.

"Nobody's safe," he said. "Get that into your head. Where this sort of thing is concerned, nobody's safe. Nobody can stay out of it!"

"I know that, Billy," I said. "I'm not arguing with you. I can see the way you were caught."

He digested that.

"I have to live here, you know, Brian," he said. "It's all very well being brave, you in your chair, but I've got to go up the Road tomorrow, and Stan will be there. He doesn't make allowances for anybody, Stanley. Not a dicky bird."

The heroics of being-in-on-the-operation had all left him. Well, he couldn't have it both ways.

Either he was a big man, outwitting the Brits for the cause of Being British, or else he was a nobody that the UDA had made use of, too scared to say no.

He knew which he was.

So did I.

I'd have to help him to forget it, or gloss over the truth, because he wasn't brave enough to be a coward.

I should never have let him talk about it.

If I had kept my mouth shut and not asked questions he could have gone on about being the big man who is part of the secret, winking and nodding when Stan called him "Billy".

It would have been better not to know. He had me scared as well, scared of knowing.

That's the way it is.

Fear is the stitch that holds the whole thing together.

You can sense it, in the beat of the drum.

I sat there long after Billy had gone to bed, thinking about my Auntie Mae and Billy, and the way their not-very-much-of-a-life-anyway was threatened at every turn. It wouldn't have taken much to make them happy – in Billy's case just his own house, his own wife, his own street; in Mae's case just Billy being happy with her, even if she didn't want to be there. And me. She needed me too, even if he didn't.

She needed me here, *now*.

She might need me more in the time to come, if Billy hit trouble and all I was thinking of was getting away, so I could live my own life out of it.

Maybe I couldn't do that.

Maybe I'd have to stay, and pay back some of the love I owed her.

A part of me kept thinking: *It's not my debt.* Another part of me knew that it was. She'd given me all that she had to give.

CHAPTER ELEVEN

I didn't see Billy the next morning. He had cleared off before I came down, which didn't displease me. It might have been a difficult enough conversation!

Duggie came in after the cornflakes.

"Big do down Cleaver Street, Hanna," he said. "The Popehead has called round to collect his belongings."

"Sean Neary?" I said.

"Aye!" he said.

He wanted to go and see what was happening, so I went with him.

There was a car parked outside the Nearys'. It wasn't his car, because Neary's car wasn't going any more. It got the side whack of the blast when the army blew the windows out of his house.

Neary had two hard men with him. They must have been brothers or cousins or something, for they both had a look of him. One of them was standing guard on the door, with his hands in his jacket, and Neary and the other one were going in and out of the house, carrying things.

Mr Malcolmson came up to us, looking cheerful.

"It'll be good to see the back of that one," he said.

"Yeah," said Duggie enthusiastically.

"People like that lower the tone of the place," Mr Malcolmson said with conviction.

Sean Neary came out of the house, carrying a big plastic laundry basket stuffed with plates and dishes. He paused at the boot of the car, and looked down the street at us, but he didn't do anything.

"I'll have a word, and speed him on his way," said Mr Malcolmson.

He marched up the street towards the car.

The lookout on the door heaved himself off the doorpost, and called something to the other one inside. The other one came out and joined him, and they moved clear of the door, and into the space fronting the gate – or where the gate had been, anyway. It was knocked skew whiff by the blast, and was over in the hedge.

"Your man Neary is on eggshells," Duggie said.

Mr Malcolmson came up to Sean Neary, and tapped him on the shoulder.

Neary had turned away, making out that he didn't see anybody coming, but he saw Mr Malcolmson well enough.

Mr Malcolmson said a few words, and then he held out his hand to Neary, as if he was going to shake hands, but Sean Neary didn't take the hand. He brushed past Mr Malcolmson and went into the house, leaving his minders watchful on the step behind him.

Mr Malcolmson came back to us, all pleased with himself.

"He won't be back, lads," he said.

"Do you think those fellas have guns?" Duggie said, looking up the street at the two minders. They were watching us. They'd given up the furniture removing.

"No," said Mr Malcolmson. "They're not hard men. The like of Sean Neary doesn't know any hard men. If he did, he wouldn't be leaving here upright. He'd be up the street in a six foot box with a hole in his head."

"You're right there," Duggie said cheerfully.

Mr Malcolmson went off about his business.

Sean Neary didn't hang about either. Between them they got the car loaded, always with one on the watch, and then one of them, the one who had been on the door, went to the car boot and took a heavy hand hammer out of it.

He disappeared back into the house.

"Hey!" Duggie said.

"It's none of our business," I said.

"Well, OK," said Duggie, doing his usual Duggie. He wasn't the one to go wading in on a three to one situation.

Some of the Young Defenders came running up the street. It wasn't by accident. Mr Malcolmson must have had them on preserve-our-neighbour-hood stand-by.

They headed for the house.

The one with the hammer was out of the house before they got near it. He made a dive for the car, which was already revving up, and off they went as fast as they could pedal, with the Young Defenders yelling after them.

"I reckon they smashed up the fittings!" Duggie said.

"Just to leave it nice for the new tenant," I said.

Then a cop car came in off the Road, and cruised down, stopping across the head of Cleaver Street. It stopped for a moment, and we could see the cops looking down towards Neary's house, where the Young Defenders were busy doing nothing, all of a sudden.

"You see that?" said Duggie. "Neary had police protection to smash up the house. Wait'll you see. They'll pick our fellas up."

But the police didn't make any move down the street. They got back in the car and drove off.

I think Duggie was disappointed.

CHAPTER TWELVE

The really nasty bits creep up on you ... I don't mean the Neary business, bashing holes in the bath and the lavatory bowl with hammers, a sort of tit for tat for them being scared off.

It was the leaflets that started it.

Val turned up with them.

They were *God's Will For Ulster* leaflets, all about her dad's next big do at the mission, and she'd told her dad she could fix up some of the delivering.

"I thought you'd be pleased," she said to Duggie. "You and Brian can do these, and you'll get two pounds a hundred, just for sticking them in people's doors."

"That's kids' stuff," Duggie said.

"It's still money," I said.

"I'd come myself, but I have to see somebody," she said, and she blushed.

I suppose I should have been sore. She was

by-the-way out with us doing the leaflets, and all it was was a cover for meeting Ronnie-the-boyfriend.

"Oh," I said. "Yeah!"

"Oh go on, Brian," she said. "*Please?*"

We ended up doing the leaflets.

We were supposed to leaflet the streets round the back.

Duggie had to do most of it, and he soon got fed up.

The fourth street we went to, he disappeared halfway down, and he turned up again out of an entry, grinning.

"Where's the leaflets?" I said, because he'd gone off with two hundred, and there were just a few in his hands when he came back.

"Delivered," he said.

"In somebody's bin?" I said.

"Yeah," he said.

"What are you going to do if one of Pastor Martin's congregation is on bin collection?" I said.

"Didn't think of that," said Duggie. "Should I go back and get them?"

"Naw," I said. The more delivering we did, the more I was going off it, and getting mad at Val for using me.

We came to some bigger houses, and that was even worse, because I couldn't get at most of the doors.

"I'm making this the final delivery!" Duggie said, and he grabbed a whole pile of leaflets out of my chair bag, and disappeared up the street.

He left me sitting there.

I reckoned I was going to bake in the sun. The arm rests on my chair get all sticky. I would have wheeled myself out of it, but there wasn't anywhere to wheel to. The sun was right overhead.

I sat there and stewed.

I was sitting, stewing, when a car turned off the Road, and pulled into the side, about two hundred yards away from me.

It was a neat little job, a Honda or one of those, I'm not much up on cars, so I don't really know.

Hicky got out of it.

Straight out of it, no pause.

He took a quick look round him, and started walking, away from me, towards the Road. The car moved away from the kerb. A youngish-looking man with a short military haircut was driving it. He went the opposite way to Hicky, and turned off into Hay Street, just as Duggie turned out of it.

"Who was that in the car?" I said, when Duggie came up to me.

"What car?" he said.

"That car that went past you," I said.

"I didn't see any car."

"Hicky just climbed out of it," I said.

"Then it was *Hicky* in the car!" Duggie said, as if he had made a big joke.

"It was some guy I don't know," I said. "Who do I not know that Hicky knows?"

Which was, of course, a daft question, but it was

110

a nagger, just the same. It seemed a funny place for Hicky to be getting put down, that's all. We were well off our own streets, and the car had been coming down the Road, that is *past* our streets ... what was the point of that?

I could think of one set of circumstances that would cover it, but I didn't want to, because of where that would lead me.

Not even Hicky would be that stupid.

"Probably he's been at it again," Duggie said cheerfully.

"Joy-riding?" I said, not thinking much of the straw I was grasping at.

"Why not? He might as well get lifted for that, as anything else. Doesn't make any difference, anyway. As soon as he gets lifted the police let him go again."

As soon as he gets lifted the police let him go again... Oh God! A man with a military haircut in a car...

"He might have held on and given us a ride," Duggie said.

I listened to him, but my mind was elsewhere, trying to cope with the Hicky problem – refusing to believe it, really, because I didn't want to believe.

I let the conversation with Duggie carry me along, and pushed the Hicky business to the back of my mind as best I could.

"I didn't know you went in motors," I said. "You can get yourself shot doing that."

"Oh no," he said. "Half the time the police never bother. They have more important things to be at."

"Half the time they do," I said. "It depends what half you're in when they catch you."

"It's all right as long as you steer clear of the road blocks," Duggie said.

There are road blocks around town, because of the IRA. It's for spot searching. They move the road blocks about, but only a half-wit would drive a stolen car into a road block, when you can see the traffic building up at one. An odd time somebody who is tight or on the glue has a go at bursting through the road blocks, usually late at night, but that is the sort of game people get killed at.

"What about Val's leaflets?" I said.

"Some in the doors, for the look of the thing," he said. "There's a few more in the bushes at Hay Street."

"What if somebody sees them?" I said anxiously. I hadn't a conscience about the leaflets, but I didn't want to get caught out either, just because Duggie hadn't the wit to find somewhere safe to dump them. There is old scrap land at the end of Hay Street that is supposed to be being turned into a community garden for the old folks, only nobody has got round to it yet. The few scrubby bushes that were there didn't sound like much of a hiding place to me.

"Who is going to poke around the bushes?" Duggie said. "It's all old carry-outs and dog dirt."

112

"Wheel us up there till I get them," I said.

"Away off," he said.

"We'll get them and dump them somewhere sensible," I said.

"Oh aye?" he said. "Like *where*?"

"Like the derelicts," I said.

"Y-e-a-h!" he said, brightening. "Nice one, Hanna."

He wheeled me up to the scrap land, parked me at Hay Street in beneath the King Billy on the gable, and into the bushes he went.

Then ...

... *crash bang* comes this police tender up the road, going like the clappers.

"Cops!" I shouted.

Duggie crouched down. It was just instinct, with both of us. They wouldn't have sent a police tender doing ninety up the road for a load of leaflets. Still, it felt as if we had been caught out.

The tender went past, and screeched round the corner and away up the Road, away from us.

Duggie came out of the bushes with the leaflets, *some* of them, anyway.

"Close shave," he said.

"They weren't after us," I said.

"I know that," he said, but he was only letting on that he did. You could tell that from the look on his face. Duggie isn't like Hicky. Duggie is dead scared of the cops, even though he has only been lifted once, for stealing lead off Henderson's roof.

113

"Well, I got them anyway," Duggie said, and he dumped the leaflets back in my chair bag, and then he went over to the kerb and had a go at getting the dog dirt off his feet.

"Every dog in the neighbourhood goes in there," he grumbled.

"Keep your feet away from me when you are pushing, because you stink!" I told him.

"Come on," he said. "Let's get rid of this junk,"

We went down to the derelicts, into number 6, and dumped the leaflets.

"This place pongs!" Duggie said.

"I wonder who lived here?" I said.

"Morrisons," Duggie said.

"Where are they now?" I said.

"The old fella died, and the woman's in the loony bin," he said.

"Is she the one...?" I said.

"Aye, that one," he said.

I remembered it well enough. She wouldn't budge when they wanted to pull the houses down. They bricked up on both sides of her, and she got on TV giving off about it. It was because she was on TV that I remembered her. I sometimes think that getting on TV is the only thing that counts round here, if you want people to remember who you are. Anyway, she got sick, and the social services carted her off in an ambulance. The same day the Public Health were in the house and they cleared the place of all her stuff, sealed up the pipes and whatnot, and bricked up her door so that she couldn't move back if she came out of hospital. Now she's dotty in a home.

"That was bloody awful," I said.

"Money talks!" Duggie said.

We were wheeling back up the road. Duggie was about to get deeply philosophical!

"There's them, and there's us, Hanna," he said. "They've got money, and we haven't. They've got jobs, and we haven't. We're the ones that get stuffed."

He made it sound like a sort of anthem, not a battle cry. He was resigned to it.

"Nobody's stuffing me," I said. "I'm not sticking round for them to do it. You stay here and get stuffed if you want to, I'm not."

"You think you're smart, Hanna," said Duggie. "But you're not as smart as you think you are."

"Oh?" I said. "What way?"

"That Val Martin for a start," he said. "I could tell you things about her. I've been asking around."

"I know all about Val," I said.

"She's only having you on," he said.

"She never had me on," I said.

"Oh aye!" he said. "Sure!"

And he called Val a few dirty names.

I didn't get answering him back, because we were distracted. As we came across the back of the flats there was a big row going on.

Neil Williamson came up to us.

"What's happening?" Duggie asked.

"The cops have lifted two from the flats," he said.

There was a group of policemen on the edge of the crowd, and two tenders. A sergeant was standing over by the flats, talking to Stan Leadbetter and Mr Malcolmson. Stan was red in the face and waving his arms about. He was trying to give the police sergeant orders and the sergeant was busy not listening.

"Who got lifted?" Duggie asked.

"Dunno," Neil said.

Ollie Leadbetter came across to us.

"*You're* all right," he said to me.

"Eh?" I said.

"Hammer Orme and the Elbow are away," he said. "Something showed up in Orme's cabbage patch!"

Then I got it.

He meant I was all right because Billy was all right. The cops hadn't lifted *him*.

"Hammer'll not open his mouth," he said. "Same goes for the Elbow."

I didn't even know who they were.

There was a kerfuffle on one of the balconies. The police were up there doing a search. One of the women started screaming for Stan.

He lit off up the stairs, with the sergeant after him. Not chasing him, they went together.

"My da will sort it out," Ollie Leadbetter said.

"Were the cops at our house?" I said.

"What would they be at your house for?"

116

Duggie asked, suddenly twigging that I was getting a lot of special attention from Ollie.

"Wise up, Duggie!" Ollie Leadbetter said. "Now's not the time to be asking questions. Just clear off and keep your heads down till my da has things sorted out. OK?"

"Right," I said.

Ollie went back into the crowd, all full of himself.

"I'm going to our house," I said.

"I'm not!" Duggie said. "I don't want to miss out on any of the action."

I wheeled away from him.

I was glad to be away. I had to be away.

Billy.

If Billy was put in jail, it would break Auntie Mae altogether. I didn't know how I could cope with Auntie Mae, but I'd have to cope, because it was down to me.

I remember thinking how odd it was that Auntie Mae was *my* responsibility now, and not the other way about. She was the one who rescued me, who looked after me, who cared for me, who loved me – legs or no legs – who lifted me and laid me and cried over me, and now it was changed.

If he got arrested.

If.

If my mum and dad hadn't gone shopping for curtains.

If ... if ... *if*...

And the mean part of me was crying that I didn't

want all this, that I wanted away to a life of my own, while the other part insisted that whether I wanted it or not, I'd got it.

That's what was going on in my head, as I went back to our house.

CHAPTER THIRTEEN

Then ... nothing happened. No cops coming for Billy, no nothing.

He arrived home about five o'clock, which is way too early for him. Don't ask me how he managed it. I didn't ask him.

He came in and slumped straight down, in front of the TV.

He was one unhappy-looking Billy.

"I'll see about food if you like," I said. It was one of Auntie Mae's late days. I usually do the cooking then, if we cook.

"Never bother," he said. "I'll go down to the chippy."

He hopped out of the chair again, and off he went.

For somebody collecting two sausage suppers he was a long time away. He must have had some interesting conversations on the journey.

Our news was just coming on the BBC when he got back.

The guns were all there, laid out in the back room of some police barrack. The police were making a big production number out of it. *And why shouldn't they*, I thought. After all, that is what they are there for.

It was rifles and ammunition mainly, with some bomb-making materials, which puzzled me a bit because our side doesn't go in much for bombs these days. Shooting people is more fun.

"Police operations are continuing and further arrests are anticipated."

No Councillor Paden or Pastor Martin for that matter. The time had come for them to adopt a low profile.

"Do you not want to see what it says on *Six Tonight*?" I said. *Six Tonight* is the Ulster Television news slot; it comes on just after the BBC local news. You can switch across and get the same story twice.

"Aye," he said. "I suppose so."

We sat and watched it all over again. Billy made a few remarks that were almost chirpy, befitting somebody with inside knowledge of something that had ended up on TV. If it had been me, I'd have been hiding under the bedclothes, or packing a bag to make a flit before the police came to collect me.

Ulster Television had nothing that the BBC hadn't already carried.

"Switch it off, Brian," the star of TV said from deep in his chair. I resisted the temptation to tell

120

him to switch it off himself, considering that he was camped right in front of it. It wasn't a moment to cross him.

"Well, you're not arrested yet, Billy," I said.

Surely if they were going to arrest him they'd have come by now?

"Aye," he said.

"Don't worry," I said, hoping to raise him a bit. "It may never happen."

"I know what I'm doing," he said. With the television off, he had reverted to looking small, the squat of his body in the chair edgily defensive.

I took his chip plate and dumped it with my own in the kitchen, and then I came back into the front room.

"What are you going to do?" I asked anxiously. The thought in my mind was that he shouldn't just sit there and wait for the police to come if they were coming. He should have been on his bike, but the thought of Billy getting up from his fireside and going on the run didn't have any feeling of reality. His small set life couldn't be disturbed that way. "Will you be arrested, do you think?" I said.

"How should I know?" he mumbled.

"You know more than I do," I said. I wanted to get it across to him that I wasn't making polite conversation. I wanted to help.

"It's the bloody van," he said. "If they know about the van, they're bound to get round to me."

I didn't say anything. I couldn't see how the police *wouldn't* know about the van. I didn't want

121

to tell him what an idiot he had been letting Stan use him and his van, just like that, out of the blue. Of course, I didn't know it *was* out of the blue. I felt it was, but I couldn't be sure.

"They found the stuff," he said. "That doesn't necessarily mean that they know how it got there."

He glanced across at me, for confirmation. I nodded.

"If they don't know how it got there, that's you in the clear," I said, "probably."

The thought seemed to grow in him, as he sat there toying with it. He brightened up perceptibly.

"In the clear," he repeated.

"Have you ever been mixed up in this sort of thing before, Billy?" I asked.

He didn't say anything, but he gave me a dirty look.

"OK," I said. "Sorry! Sorry I spoke."

"You talk too much anyway," he said, and then I got a second dirty look, uneasier than the first, which should have given me a foretaste of what was coming, but it didn't.

"Why do you think I wasn't lifted with the Hammer and the Elbow, Brian?" he said.

"Because they don't know about the van," I said. "They got the stuff, but they don't know how it was moved."

"The police knew where to look," he said. "They went straight to it in Hammer's garden. They had their spades with them and all. No messing about like on their visit to the band rooms."

122

"Why didn't they find the stuff in the band rooms?" I said.

"Because the stuff wasn't in the band rooms!" he said.

I let that one hover for a while, while I worked at it.

"The guns were in the mission hall itself?" I said.

"Why not?" he said.

Well, I was sure that Pastor Martin or Val could have told him why not, unless...

"Did Pastor Martin *know*?" I asked.

"How should I know if the pastor knew?" he said impatiently. "It makes no odds to me. It is the here and now that is bothering me, the same way it is bothering a lot of people round here. The here and now of it is that somebody, *somebody*, tipped the wink to the cops or the army. The police didn't come galloping up with spades and shovels and head straight for the spot in the cabbage patch without *somebody* tipping them off."

He was watching me very closely, waiting for a reaction.

I suddenly got the drift I was meant to get.

"Ah, Billy!" I said.

The sympathy for him which had been building up inside me began to fade.

"Well?" he said.

"I didn't even know where the stuff was!" I said. I could still hardly credit what he was thinking.

"Keep your voice down!" he said, as if I had been shouting.

Billy thought that *I* had tipped off the Security Forces about the stuff.

"I don't want the neighbours in on this," he said, and he got up and closed the door.

"Listen, Billy," I said. "You know and I know that I'm no God and Ulster enthusiast. Everybody round here knows that…"

"It's because *they* know that, that *you* could be in trouble," he said.

He meant it. Somebody must have said something to him when he was out getting the chips.

"Is somebody saying I am an informer?" I said. "Let's have it straight out."

"I'll tell you what they might think," he said. "They might think there were three on the job, me and Hamilton Orme and the Elbow, and two of us got picked up. They might think, 'Why was Billy Moore let off the hook?' when I'm the one the police can link with the van, easy as easy."

"Oh," I said.

"Did you do it, Brian?" Billy asked.

"No," I said.

I didn't tell him that I knew who had done it. I didn't tell him because I didn't want him to know.

It was *Hicky*. Hicky and the stranger in the car, some army undercover man or special kind of cop, dropping him off in a sidestreet where he wouldn't be recognized. It had to be Hicky. As-soon-as-he-gets-lifted-the-police-let-him-go-again Hicky, black-mailed into it by the threat of going to prison, and kept going by pay-outs from some informer-fund.

124

Hicky hadn't even the intelligence to invent a credible story to account for the money he had.

I wasn't going to tell Billy, because Billy would tell the UDA ... if Stan didn't know already!

If he didn't know, he must have *suspected* and suspicion is usually enough.

"You would be better telling me if it *was* you, than telling the paramilitaries," Billy said. "I would help you."

Maybe he cared more about me than he had ever let on.

"You've got no sense of self-preservation, Billy," I said.

"What?"

"Never mind," I said.

My big thought was that I had to get out, fast, and warn Hicky, because if I had worked out that he was the infomer, then it was almost certain that Stan would work it out too.

"Brian?" Billy said. "Where are you going?"

"Out!" I said.

"Brian...?"

I left him Brian-ing me. I had to get to Hicky before somebody else did.

CHAPTER FOURTEEN

I suppose I knew it wasn't going to work.

I went round to Hicky's house and one of his sisters opened the door. I don't know which one. She had a tight dress and yellow plastic curlers in her hair. Her eyes were all puffy.

"What do you want?" she said.

"Is Sammy in?" I said. Sammy is Hicky's name.

"No," she said.

"Do you know where he is?"

"No," she said.

"Who is it?" somebody yelled from inside.

"Young Brian Hanna!" she yelled back.

"Tell him to go away!"

"Go away," she said.

She shut the door firmly in my face.

I was stuck in my chair, not knowing what to make of it.

Mrs Williamson came across the street to me.

"Brian!" she said. "Come away from there."

"Eh?" I said.

"Don't be disturbing them," she said. "Come on!" and she grabbed my chair and started wheeling.

"What's going on?" I said, as we crossed the road. I don't even know Mrs Williamson properly. She's just one of the faces you see around and know, sort of.

"Sammy Hicky is away," she said. "Do you understand me?"

"No," I said.

"They came for him in a van," she said.

"Oh," I said. "*Who* came?"

"I don't know who came," she said. She came round from the back of the chair, letting go the handles. "Nobody knows," she said. "Just some men. They weren't from round here."

"Oh," I said.

"Do you know why?" she said.

I shook my head.

"Nobody knows," she said. "But they took him away."

"Right," I said.

"So don't you be disturbing that poor woman," she said.

"No, Mrs Williamson," I said. "I'll go away now."

I went.

I should go to the police, that was my thought, but I knew it was already too late to go to the police. The family would probably have done that themselves, in desperation. I had nothing to add, nothing that would help.

Maybe they would just beat him.

I ended up down by the swings, with my head resting on the railings, whacked inside and whacked out, trying to cope with what had happened, but unable to.

Then Val showed up.

"Brian?" she said. "Brian? Penny for them, Brian? Are you mad at me, Brian?"

"No," I said.

"Well then, what's this?" she said.

"What's what?"

There was a long pause. I *was* mad at her, because I didn't want to have to cope with her, with the Hicky thing bubbling all over me. But she was really concerned for me. She huddled down beside the railing, with her back against it, and her big, worried face turned up towards me.

"Brian?" she said. "What is it, Brian? You can tell me."

I couldn't.

It wasn't Hicky. There was nothing I could do to help Hicky now. It was to do with Billy and my Auntie Mae, and their little house ... *our* little house.

"Brian?" she said. "Brian? Take you wheelies, shall I?"

"No," I said. Then: "Yes, do that!"

We bump-bump-bumped along and I thought I would have to find a way to tell her about Hicky, but I couldn't, and I decided I wouldn't because it

128

might not be as bad as I thought it was. It might not happen. He might get away with a beating.

I felt close to Val, which was odd, because we shouldn't have been able to communicate at all. Her mind was packed full of God and hellfire, and a thing like what happened to Hicky was the by-product of thinking that way. I didn't want to expose her to that. In a way we were never able to communicate, but in another way we did.

I had to say something, anything.

I told her about the leaflets. Another day, another time, without the Hicky-knowledge hanging over me, the thing I couldn't bring myself to talk about, I would have known better. The leaflets meant nothing as far as I was concerned, in the shadow of all that was threatening me. But they were her leaflets, and the part of me that was still functioning on that level was worried in case she got into a row about them, and then turned round and said I had cheated her. Most of my mind was with Hicky, trying to cope with what they might to do him, and another part was involved in the leaflet thing. I couldn't let Val get into a row when she was trying so hard to be kind and help me.

"I'm very sorry, Val," I said.

"Oh help!" she said. "You're going to get me into trouble." She looked and sounded as if she meant it, too.

"If Dad finds out, Mummy will guess what has been going on," she said. "Mummy will tell Dad about Ronnie. He doesn't know about Ronnie."

Maybe Hicky will just get a beating, I was thinking.

"Your dad's not going to know about Ronnie," I said.

Sometimes they use planks with nails in them. Sometimes they use baseball bats.

"Yes, he will! He will!" She was very agitated, bumping me clumsily along the road, not really looking where she was going, scared stiff of Mummy and Daddy finding out.

They might just break his arms and legs, or take a poke at his kneecaps with a power drill.

"Brian?" she said, sounding pained.
"We could go and get the leaflets," I said. "Pick them up now, and go round tomorrow delivering them."

Hicky could be dead by now.

"Yeah!" she said. "Yeah! We could, couldn't we? You're brilliant, Brian."

I wonder what a gun would feel like, up against my brain?

"We'll go and get the leaflets then," I said.

I wonder what the bullet would feel like, going in?

"Your mummy won't know," I said.

We went to the derelicts, Val hurrying along in her clumpy shoes and me bumping in front of her, trying not to think.

I couldn't tell her.

What was – *might be* – happening to Hicky was a dark thing inside me. I couldn't bring myself to talk about it.

I talked about Mummy not knowing about Ronnie, instead, because that was the important thing.

"You want to stay outside?" I said, when we got to the derelicts. "I can wheel in by myself."

"Don't be silly," she said.

So in we went.

No Hicky.

The leaflets were there all right, but somebody had done a dance on them. They were spread right across the old broken-up floor.

"I didn't leave them like that," I said.

She was down on the floor scrabbling for them as if they were gold dust, or fragments from the tablets off the Mount.

I wheeled myself out of her way.

I was in front of her, by the bricked-up window, and I glanced up at the hole in the ceiling, which was behind her, where the staircase used to be.

I was looking straight into the barrel of a gun.

There was a man there.

He looked like a soldier, a Brit.

He was wearing combat uniform, with his face blackened.

He grinned at me.

He wagged the barrel of the gun, as if to say that he wasn't going to fire it, but he might.

Then he jerked his head towards the hole we'd come in through, and moved back from the gap in the ceiling, and out of my line of vision.

I remember thinking how strange it was that he didn't make any sound. If I hadn't seen him I wouldn't have known he was there.

"That's it," Val said. "Stuff those in your bag."

She dumped the leaflets in my lap.

"Let's get out of here," she said. "I don't like this old place. It's weird."

Then we were out on the street again.

"You're very quiet," she said.

"Yes," I said.

"I really don't like it in there, Brian," she said.

"Don't you ever say you were near it," I said. "Just in case."

"In case *what*?" she said.

If I tell her she'll want to tell her Dad, I thought.

Probably the man was a soldier, a Brit.

Maybe he wasn't.

Our side, or theirs?

A man with a gun in a derelict house, all dressed up like a commando. An observation point perhaps, or a stake-out for some yet-to-happen killing. We'd walked into the middle of it, and walked out again. We hadn't been killed.

Val didn't know that it had happened.

I didn't tell her. She pushed me up the road,

chattering all the way. I was busy working on whether or not I ought to go to the police, because if the man in the house wasn't from the Security Forces somebody might get killed.

I didn't go to the police.

I just bump-bump-bumped along the pavement in my chair and let Val talk, and waited and waited and waited for the image of the man to burn itself out of my brain, but it didn't.

Probably he wasn't a killer.

He must have been a Brit.

And they're on my side ... that was my thought. Supposed to be. But the Brits or the cops or somebody had taken Hicky and used his shop-lifting and his joy-riding to blackmail him with the thought of going to prison. They'd paid him for information about what went on in our streets, when they knew selling it could kill him. The Security Forces are the good guys. They're not supposed to do that. I could understand why they had done it, but I couldn't forgive them.

I don't think the man with the gun and the blacked-up face had anything to do with Hicky, despite the fact that the derelict was one of Hicky's hidey-holes. I don't think he had anything to do with Hicky, because by that time Hicky was already dead.

A woman out with her dog found him in the bushes at Hay Street, where the community garden for the old folk is going to be.

Hicky didn't die there.

He died somewhere else, local, in one of the little houses or somebody's coal-shed, and then they dumped him in a rubbish sack, in the bushes, for the dogs to sniff at.

There was a lot of blood in the sack.

CHAPTER FIFTEEN

It kept fine for the funeral.

I went with my un-arrested Uncle Billy, all boiled up in his Sunday suit. We walked along behind the hearse with Hicky's coffin in it. They had Hicky's band hat on top of the coffin, with his gloves neatly folded, and his fife.

"I wonder how many of the mourners know who killed him," I said.

"You keep your mouth shut," Billy said.

Afterwards, Duggie and Val and I sloped off on our own, to the park.

"I don't think it was our ones," Duggie said. "I don't believe it was them."

"It was a punishment killing, Duggie," I said.

"That doesn't mean it was Protestants," said Duggie stubbornly. "It could have been the Brits, trying to stir things up and discredit the Loyalists."

"I don't care who killed him," Val said quietly. She had started crying again.

She was down in our house crying a lot, in the days before the funeral. Auntie Mae kept making her cups of tea.

There were lots of people in the park, kids on playschemes and people walking their dogs and wheeling babies about in pushchairs. Everything was normal and unchanged, except that Hicky was dead, but that didn't seem to fizz on the people in the park. An army patrol on the Road went by, single file, spaced out strategically, with the leader talking into his radio, and a helicopter high overhead. It hung up there in the beam of the sun and whirred at us, waiting for action below.

There wasn't any.

I sat in my chair, looking at the people.

I couldn't cope with the fact that the people who did that to Hicky were probably out in the sunshine with us, licking their ice creams or bouncing their babies.

They'd have cleaned the blood off the walls of the room they killed him in before coming out of course, to keep it looking nice for the neighbours.

And washed their hands.

I felt that we were washing him off our hands as well, Val and Duggie and I, sitting in the hot sun on the grassy slope above the river, and talking about nothing, when we talked, which wasn't often.

Duggie was the first to go. He went off home, and that left me and Val.

I was thinking about her leaflets.

There were some of them under the sack when they found Hicky. The blood must have trickled out on to them. They were sodden with it. I didn't tell Val that. There would have been no point. Hicky couldn't have read the big words in the leaflets anyway.

"I've got to go, Brian," she said, getting up from the ground, and knocking the dried grass off her clothes. "Will I wheel you back?"

"I'll manage myself," I said.

She didn't argue.

She just walked off, her back stiff as a poker, face pale.

That left me to go home to Auntie Mae.

"Brian?" she said, when I came in.

She was all on her own, in the kitchen. I don't know where Billy was. I was glad he wasn't there, because I wanted her on her own.

"Brian?" she said again.

Then...

"Don't cry, Brian," she said.

She was nearly crying herself.

I wasn't crying just for Hicky. It was for us, all of us, and what we'd come to.

"We're a fine pair!" she said.

"I'm sorry," I said. "I'm supposed to be making you feel better, and I can't do it, because I'm not able to."

"The cry will do you good," she said.

"Don't tell Billy I was crying," I said.

"Och, him!" she said.

Then she made some tea, and we sat a while in the kitchen and drank it, and we talked about Hicky and the times we had with him, but we didn't talk about what had happened to him, because we didn't want to talk about that.

"So now there's only us," she said.

"And Billy," I said.

"Some of the time," she said. "Billy … well, Billy is Billy, isn't he? He won't change now. It is too late. He is the way he is, and I can like it or lump it."

"You wouldn't go away from here?" I said.

"Sheffield?" she said. "No way."

"I won't be going away either then," I said.

She didn't say anything.

I sat there thinking that's me committed, and why did I say that, when maybe I will change my mind tomorrow or the day after or the next time someone gets shot?

"I had it all planned out, the going away," I said. "I had it all planned out for after my A levels."

"And you've changed your mind," she said. It wasn't a question. It was a statement. She didn't sound too happy about it.

"I haven't got a big answer for everything all of a sudden," I said. "That would be too simple. I'm staying because I think I ought to stay. If I go, and all the others who think like me go, what'll happen to the people who are left?"

"Like me and Billy," she said.

"Yes," I said, but it wasn't just personal. It went

138

deeper than that, our house, our street, our place, the people in the park ... even the ones who did what they did to Hicky, and the IRA who shot eldest sons in Fermanagh. They were one bag, take them or leave them.

"You don't have to stay because of me," Auntie Mae said. "You aren't responsible for other people. You don't owe anybody anything."

But she was wrong.

I am responsible. That's why I am staying here.

NOTES FOR *STARRY NIGHT*, *FRANKIE'S STORY* AND *THE BEAT OF THE DRUM*

I have been asked to explain some of the terms used in these books to help readers who are not familiar with the Northern Ireland situation. These notes are not intended to be comprehensive, nor can they possibly deal with the finer points of Irish history or politics. People, events and organizations who don't appear in the books don't make it into the notes either. The intent is simply to make the problems faced by Kathleen, Frankie and Brian easier to understand.

HISTORY AND GEOGRAPHY

Ireland – The island of Ireland is made up of thirty-two counties. Historically the country, which was ruled by the British for many centuries, was divided into four provinces, one of which is Ulster.

Ulster – The province of Ulster consists of nine counties. When partition of Ireland was imposed by the British in 1921 after the War of Independence, three of the nine Ulster counties were part of the newly created Irish Free State which later became the Republic of Ireland.

The *Republic of Ireland* is an independent country with a large Catholic majority.

Northern Ireland consists of the remaining six counties of the province of Ulster. It has a Protestant majority. At present it remains part of the *United Kingdom of Great Britain and Northern Ireland*.

GLOSSARY

Terms used when speaking of both sides:

Paramilitary – In present-day Northern Ireland this term is used to describe terrorist organizations, either Protestant or Catholic, who are prepared to kill to further their own political ends.

Terms used when speaking of the Irish side:

Catholic – The religion of the vast majority of the population of Ireland as a whole, and of a substantial minority of the population of Northern Ireland.

Nationalist – Those who desire a thirty-two-county united Ireland. Many, but by no means all, Catholics in Northern Ireland are Nationalists.

SDLP – The Social Democrat and Labour Party. The main Nationalist Party in Northern Ireland. The SDLP supports the unification of Ireland by democratic means, but is totally opposed to the use of force to achieve this end.

Republican Movement – The minority within the Nationalist community in Northern Ireland who very largely support the use of armed force to achieve a united Ireland.

Republican Areas – Areas regarded by Protestants as strongholds of Catholics who support the Republican Movement.

Fenian – Historically an Irish warrior. An abusive term when used by Protestants, meaning Catholic and implying rebel.

IRA – Historically the paramilitary wing of the Republican Movement.

The Provisional IRA/Provos/ Provies – The main paramilitary wing of present-day Republicanism, which was initially a splinter group of the IRA, but has now virtually superseded that organization. The term IRA is often used to describe the Provisional IRA.

Sinn Fein – A political party which supports the aims and ideals of the Provisional IRA. Believed by many Unionists to be one and the same with that organization.

Gerry Adams – President of Sinn Fein.

Terms used when speaking of the British side:

Protestant – The religion of the majority of the population of Northern Ireland, many of whom are of Scots and English descent.

Unionists – Those who support the union of Great Britain with Northern Ireland. Many, but by no means all, Protestants in Northern Ireland are Unionists.

RUC – The Royal Ulster Constabulary. The police force in Northern Ireland is largely Protestant. Attempts are being made, not very successfully, to redress this imbalance. Catholics who join the RUC are very vulnerable to Republican attack. Protestant paramilitaries who oppose government policy regard the RUC as traitors to their cause.

UDR – The Ulster Defence Regiment was a locally recruited and mainly Protestant unit of the British Army. Now replaced by the Royal Irish Regiment.

Loyalists – The hard edge of Protestant Unionism. Many, but by no means all, Loyalists are prepared to use force to maintain the union with Great Britain, and some are willing to fight the British to prove it.

UDA – The Ulster Defence Association. A Protestant organization with some political and some paramilitary overtones.

UFF – Ulster Freedom Fighters. A Protestant paramilitary organization, believed by many to be part of the UDA.

UVF – Ulster Volunteer Force. A Protestant paramilitary organization.

The Orange Order –
A Protestant religious
organization with political and
charitable overtones. It has
considerable influence within
Unionist politics.

The Twelfth – 12 July.
The Orange Order's annual
celebration of the victory of the
Protestant King William of
Orange (King Billy) over the
Catholic King James II at the
Battle of the Boyne in 1690.
Orange Order Marches take
place all over Northern Ireland
and many fiery speeches are
made.

"The Sash" – "The Sash my
Father Wore" is an Orange
Order marching song. The sash
referred to in the song is a
form of collarette worn by
Orangemen on parade.

The Ulster Red Hand flag –
The Red Hand is the traditional
symbol of Ulster.